BLUE DEATH

BLUE DEATH

LILLIAN O'DONNELL

G. P. PUTNAM'S SONS ▼ NEW YORK

G. P. PUTNAM'S SONS
Publishers Since 1838
a member of
Penguin Putnam Inc.
200 Madison Avenue
New York, NY 10016

Copyright © 1998 by Lillian O'Donnell

Library of Congress Cataloging-in-Publication Data

O'Donnell, Lillian.
Blue death / by Lillian O'Donnell.
p.   cm.
ISBN 0-399-14367-X
I. Title.
PS3565.D59B58   1998   97-47589 CIP
813' .54—dc21

Printed in the United States of America

1   3   5   7   9   10   8   6   4   2

This book is printed on acid-free paper. ∞

Book design by Gretchen Achilles

BLUE DEATH

CHAPTER 1

▼ It was early June and already the city hunkered down under threat of another hurricane. Just a few hours before it was due to strike, the experts downgraded it to a tropical disturbance. Nevertheless, gale winds howled, lashing trees and driving the rain in sheets against the plate-glass windows of the elegant stores on Fifth Avenue that hadn't thought it worthwhile to board them up. They flouted nature's power and would pay for it. At 11:55, the lights flickered in lower Manhattan, then flickered again, and finally went out and stayed out. Upper Manhattan and Queens were next to go dark, followed in quick succession by Staten Island, Brooklyn, and the Bronx. Power was restored at four A.M. in the same sequence. Most people were asleep. Detective first grade Stewart Schiff of the Internal Affairs Bureau was one of them. But his sleep was permanent.

Schiff lay sprawled on the sofa of his Greenwich Village walk-up, the barrel of his .38 S and W service revolver in his mouth, index finger curled around the trigger, the back of his head blown out.

Detective Schiff lived alone. His wife, Irene, had divorced him three months before. He had few friends on the job, and the nature of his work limited his outside interests and attachments. He lay in a pool of his own blood for three days before the building super, nagged by complaints about the foul odor emanating from the apartment, came looking for him.

The first radio motor patrols on the scene had responded to such calls many times before. There were no surprises given the conditions: high temperature, closed windows, and gas from a decomposing body. They came prepared with chemicals to counteract the fumes and wore surgical masks that covered mouths and noses. Still, the stench was so severe they retched violently and had to flee. Once the windows had been opened and the air had cleared somewhat, the uniforms tried a second time. In a matter of seconds they took a quick look around, searched the body for ID, and even this was almost too much. They got out a second time, lurching down the stairs and out to the street, where they used a public phone to notify Internal Affairs that one of their detectives had blown his brains out. They worded it differently, of course.

The sergeant at IA who took the complaint offered to make the routine notifications, which included advising the homicide unit that would be carrying the case.

In due course, Detective Stewart Schiff's death was included in the summary of the day's events prepared by the Police Commissioner's top aide, Chief James Felix, and placed on the PC's desk each morning.

Neither man made much of it. There had been a couple of these sad events recently, the only cloud in the new PC's blue sky.

Everything was looking good for Commissioner Peter Lundy. According to statistics, crime in the city was down dramatically. It seemed Lundy was right when he insisted the "quality of life" had a direct effect on overt violence. If you cleaned up the subways and washed away the graffiti, if you controlled the panhandlers, stopped them from accosting shoppers for instance, the streets and the trains would cease to seem and to be quite so threatening. Once the ordinary citizen saw himself protected from the minor incursions on his rights, he would be more likely to trust the system to protect him from major assault.

Mayor Relkin supported his new PC enthusiastically. Why not? His theory was working.

A proposed change in the law would permit the victim of a crime to testify in court as to his feelings, to describe the trauma he suffered during the commission of the crime. In some states the suspect's record was actually admissible evidence. It was almost a new age.

The cops on the beat were regaining respect.

So why were they killing themselves?

Granted, policing was stressful work that affected each man and woman in blue in a different way. Some developed a nervous disorder. Others turned to drinking or drugs. Then the path forked: they became criminals themselves, or put an end to lives of misery. There were many ways of doing that. Lately, they had taken to blowing their brains out with their own service revolvers. There was no doubt that death came by invitation.

But why now? Peter Lundy asked himself over and over again. Why now, when they should all be basking in the glow of success, in the approval of the public, why were these men killing themselves?

Peter Lundy was a former lawyer turned professor. He affected the characteristic tweeds and carried a pipe which he never lit. His hair was a faded blond and his eyes a bright blue. He had married one of his students six months after she went to work for him, at which time she was three months pregnant. They now had two children, a boy and a girl. The marriage was a happy one.

Upon appointment, the new police commissioner had inherited a smoothly functioning department from his predecessor, John Jasper, and had been wise enough not to tamper with it. He believed it was free of corruption and didn't want to learn otherwise. Considered an expert in the field of criminal justice, Professor Lundy had taught at John Jay College, and had written three books on the subject. At fifty-one, he was sedentary but believed he was in good health despite carrying more weight than his doctor approved of. He enjoyed good food and drink and indulged himself, disregarding his doctor's cautions. He was prone to sudden flushes which he refused to take seriously.

Despite his lack of experience running any enterprise similar to the NYPD, Lundy was confident of his capabilities. At this particular moment, however, in these circumstances, he wasn't sure what he should do. He himself had little pity for these police suicides. They were losers, cowards who left family and friends to deal with whatever problem they hadn't been able to bear themselves. The sudden death of a police officer triggered a series of standard official responses expected both by the public and by the cops. Usually, someone of top rank visited the scene. Next came the obligatory sympathy call on the widow or next of kin. If death came in the line of duty, there was the pomp of an inspector's funeral—no matter what the rank of the deceased. But when a cop died by his own hand . . . What would his predecessor have done? Lundy asked himself.

Unfortunately the former PC was not available for consultation. Jasper had retired and was living on his boat in Fort Lauderdale. Putting in a call to him would only underscore his own uncertainty, the new PC decided. He pressed the button that connected him to Chief Felix.

James Felix was a three-star chief. Six foot two, solidly built, he was neither fat nor lean; call him substantial. He made a point of keeping fit, but was not obsessive about it. He took some sort of exercise each day. Sometimes it was a run through Battery Park in the morning before work. If the weather was bad he'd work out in his local gym, or play a game of squash. He was fifty-one, the same age as the new PC, and would have looked younger except for his thick shock of white hair. He had penetrating green eyes, but needed glasses to read the newspaper or other fine print. He had been married to Sally Hendricks, a former actress, for twenty-two years and expected to be married to her for another twenty-two. Their only disappointment was that they had no children.

Three years ago, Felix had been offered the appointment to Chief of Uniformed Forces, and with it his fourth star. He turned it down. He had spent his entire professional life in the detective division and it was his dream to end his career as Chief of Detectives, a post currently held, as it had been for many years, by Luis Deland. Deland was an old friend and one Felix had no intention of easing out of his job. He continued to serve as Deland's executive assistant and waited—a Cadillac doing the work of a Ford.

Then Peter Lundy came on. Lundy was experienced in evaluating men. He spotted Felix, understood his worth and wanted him. He suggested, then requested that Felix serve him as he was serving Deland. It was considered a big opportunity. Even Deland urged Jim Felix to accept.

Felix's office was on the fourteenth floor of One Police Plaza, the "Big Building," just down the hall from the PC. All he had to do was pick up the memo pertaining to yesterday's events and walk a few steps. He tapped at the door and went in.

"He just called me," Felix told Doris Kampinsky, Lundy's civilian secretary—his third in the six months since he took office. This one looked like she might last.

She nodded. "I know." And waved him on.

"Good morning, Commissioner."

"Morning, Chief." Lundy indicated Felix should take his usual place opposite him. "I've been looking over yesterday's incident list. About this latest suicide . . . Has a motive been established?"

"Not yet," Felix replied. He was surprised Lundy should fix on that when there were other high attention grabbers: a drive-by shooting of an eight-year-old girl while she slept in her bed; a threat to blow up the Fifty-ninth Street Bridge, followed by the bridge's shutdown for three hours and a river-to-river traffic jam; and the arrest of another Central Park rapist. These were cases that had already captured the attention of both the public and the media. It was to Lundy's credit that the NYPD was performing well.

"Who's carrying?" the PC wanted to know.

"Frank Tarentino, out of Homicide South."

"I don't know him."

"He's a good man," Felix assured him. "Maybe a little young, but he knows his way around. He was largely responsible for the break in the Gillespie case. You can rely on him."

"That so?" The PC was thoughtful; he produced his pipe and fiddled with it. "We've got a sensitive situation here, Chief. Another blue suicide. What kind of spin are the media putting on this one?"

There was a Commissioner of Public Relations, usually a civilian, with the specific function of handling such matters. Apparently, Lundy wanted the police slant.

"As far as I know, they're playing it down."

"Good. We'll do the same."

Felix waited.

"On the other hand, we shouldn't appear lacking in compassion. So maybe you should go over there and take a look."

"At the crime scene? It's been compromised by now. To start with, the body wasn't discovered for three days. The process of decomposition was well under way. Unauthorized persons have tramped through the premises. It will not yield useful evidence," Felix pointed out.

"Well then, talk to Tarentino. Find out what he's got. Talk to the deceased's friends, to the guys that worked with him."

"That would be at Internal Affairs."

Lundy threw him a sharp look. "We're all supposed to be working together toward the same goal. Are you intimating they won't cooperate?"

"No, nothing like that." Felix was quick to dismiss the idea. "Only that they're jealous of their reputation."

"This is the third time in the past three months that a cop has killed himself for no apparent reason."

"Right."

"When somebody, anybody, puts the barrel of a gun in his mouth and spatters his brains all over the walls, there has to be a reason, damn it! Is it a phase of the moon? What? I want to know. When three men do it, one after the other, I have to know."

▼ Though he had downplayed the value of examining the Schiff suicide scene, Jim Felix decided to take a look after all. Monday's storm had been followed by a spell of good weather. The sun was out; the air was refreshing. The Schiff apartment was within walking distance and Felix hadn't had his morning run.

A woman answered when Jim Felix rang the super's bell at the five-story brownstone. She was about fifty pounds overweight, he thought, and she jiggled when she walked. She had to bend over and squint when he opened his shield case for her to see. She appeared neither impressed by his rank nor interested in why he wanted to look at Detective Schiff's apartment.

"Do you mind if I don't go up with you? The elevator's out of order and my arthritis is killing me."

"No problem," Felix assured her, and taking the keys she handed him, started for the back stairs.

Detective Schiff's two rooms and kitchenette looked out on a so-called "garden," which was actually nothing more than a rear alley whose hard-packed, rancid soil could sustain only a single stunted tree not yet in full leaf. The long, narrow rooms with their high ceilings and drab furnishings repeated the theme of a lonely and barren life. Schiff had possessed what he needed and no more. Felix went through his closet and chest of drawers. A great deal could be learned from how a person dressed, particularly the opinion he had of himself. Did he care what kind of image he presented, what impression he made? Was he ordinary, sloppy, or sharp in his thinking? Up-to-date or behind the times? From what hung in Schiff's closet Felix deduced he'd been conservative and careful of how he spent his money, did not participate in any sport. The most telling thing was that the clothes were still there, that no one had cared enough to come around and dispose of them. Probably the Detectives Endowment Association would take care of that, and the funeral arrangements as well.

The scraping of a key in the lock of the outer door caught Felix's attention. Whoever it was was having trouble making it work, indicating he didn't come here often. As he started over to help, the would-be entrant lost patience and kicked the door open, plunging directly into his arms.

"Are you all right?"

"I think so."

She was in her late thirties, small and thin, too thin, almost unhealthily so, at least to Felix's way of thinking. She had a pixie face with a pointed chin, lank blond hair that hung straight and loose, and bangs reaching to her eyebrows, which she brushed off to one side with a self-conscious gesture that was probably habitual.

"That lock should have been fixed months ago. I told Stewart, but as long as his key worked . . ." She shrugged. "May I ask what you're doing here?"

"Police." Felix flipped open his shield case.

She studied it. "Chief," she observed. "That's important."

"Sometimes."

"You're being modest, I'm sure." Her light gray eyes were wide. "What are you doing here?"

"I have to ask you the same thing."

"I'm Irene Schiff. Stewart's wife. Or I was. We divorced three months ago."

"I'm very sorry," Felix said.

Irene Schiff sighed. "I came to sort through his things and to dispose of them. Not that there's much left." With a sweep of her right arm, she indicated the sparsely furnished room. "I feel bad. I had no idea how Stewart was living. I told Detective Tarentino I had no idea Stewart took the divorce so seriously. I mean, we had no life together. We were strangers eating at the same table and sharing the same bed. I thought the divorce didn't matter to him one way or the other. In fact, I thought he was glad of it." She lifted one shoulder in disavowal of responsibility, and her face twitched like that of a little girl explaining to her mother how the vase happened to slip out of her hands.

"You think he was despondent over the divorce and that's why he shot himself?" Felix asked.

"What else? He had no family; his last relative, a distant cousin in Vancouver, died a year ago. Working at the Bureau . . . Well, you know what that's like."

"Suppose you tell me what it was like for Stewart."

She considered. "When he first took it on, Stewart was very uncomfortable. He felt like he was spying on friends, he said. But he got used to it."

"Did you see each other after the divorce?"

"Hardly at all. He called a few times. It was always with regard to some detail—a bill to be paid, repairs to the house we were trying to sell, but really he wanted to get together. I didn't see the point, so I would turn him down."

"You didn't live here when you were married?"

"No way." Irene Schiff shook her head. "Stewart moved in here when we broke up."

"So in your opinion he was depressed by the separation?"

"I'm afraid he was."

"Since you say you didn't see much of each other after the divorce, on what do you base that opinion?"

She hesitated a long while before answering. Her lower lip trembled and her eyes filled.

"He stalked me! He told me he regretted not contesting the divorce and he warned me he could never let another man have me."

"Was there another man?"

She dropped her head so that the curtain of her hair hid her entire face. "Only in his imagination," she murmured.

Felix's face was grave. "Did you report this threat to the police?"

"With him working for IA? How far would I have got?"

"Did you tell Detective Tarentino?"

"No."

"Why not?"

"Same reason."

▼ Felix left Irene Schiff to the sad, self-imposed, and guilt-ridden task of sorting and packing the dead man's effects, and headed back to One Police Plaza. On the way he used his cell phone to call his office.

As the PC's top aide, Jim Felix had his own staff, composed mainly of civilians but headed by Police Officer Paula Lawson, a young woman a year out of the Police Academy. Paula had graduated in the top of her class. Her rank was in that nebulous area between patrol officer and detective. She was in her early thirties, a natural brunette with large, hazel eyes: attractive but not a head turner. She worked in plain clothes and at Chief Felix's hours, which meant she had a more or less steady schedule of nine to five with weekends off, a rare perk in the department. However, Paula Lawson had not joined the force to be a secretary, and Chief Felix did not treat her like one. He allowed her to observe an investigation from the inside, from beginning to end. The Chief kept no secrets from her. She idolized him.

"Reach out for Detective Frank Tarentino," Felix ordered. "I want him in my office with everything he's got on the Schiff suicide. Forthwith."

CHAPTER 2

▼ The lights in Detective Kevin Douglas's newly completed basement rumpus room were all on. He had done the entire job himself and was justifiably proud of the result. The room featured knotty pine paneling, a bar, and a giant thirty-one-inch television set. A big hockey game was scheduled at Madison Square Garden that night and Douglas had invited his buddies and their wives or girlfriends to celebrate the completion of the project which had kept him occupied for nearly two years. The men would watch the game downstairs while the women would spend the evening upstairs with Ellen Douglas and the pay-per-view of their choice.

At ten after seven, the doorbell of the modest frame house in Howard Beach started ringing. Ellen greeted their friends and herded them into the small front room with its old, rickety, mismatched furniture—donations from parents and relatives at the time they bought the house, and all of which was supposed to be replaced. Somehow, for one reason or another—as the babies came (four) and the medical bills mounted, and the car broke down, and on and on and on—they never got around to it.

"Kevin's downstairs putting the last touches," Ellen told them, to explain why the drinks weren't being passed around.

A murmur indicated they understood. Kevin Douglas was known to be a good and expansive host, while Ellen found those duties onerous. The guests that night were either cops who worked with Douglas or neighbors. They all knew each other and had plenty to gossip about while Ellen went upstairs to check on the children.

She had been a pretty child and a pretty woman, accustomed to admiration. It had given her a glow which was gone now, replaced by disappointment. It showed in her sallow face, in the dark circles under her eyes, the sagging chin. It showed in the carelessness of her dress.

Ellen and Kevin had been childhood sweethearts going back to grammar school. In high school he had been a football star, she a cheerleader. They were separated for a brief period after graduation while he tried out for the pros and she studied to be a nurse. He didn't make it. She was almost glad, because she'd been afraid that in the environment of pro sports there would be too many temptations and she would lose him. However, she succeeded and got her certificate and a choice of jobs. Kevin was embarrassed that she should be working while he was not. He made sure she'd never know it.

When he joined the force, they both thought they'd found the solution. But while Kevin thrived—he was an able officer with a drawerful of commendations to prove it—Ellen bent under the drudgery of bearing four children over eight years. And now a fifth was on the way.

Quietly, not wanting to draw attention, Dave Hinkley, Kevin's partner, intercepted Ellen. He drew her over to the dining room where they could be alone. The china clock on the serving table chimed the half hour.

Dave Hinkley was a thoughtful, quiet man, outwardly stolid but in actuality a man of dreams. His triangular face was framed by dark wavy hair. He lacked his partner's flair, though some said he was lacking in courage. In fact, what he lacked was Kevin's impulsiveness, and because he studied a dangerous situation before acting, his courage was the greater.

"Game time is seven thirty-five," Hinkley reminded Ellen. "You know Kevin never misses J.D.'s and Sam's pregame remarks. Are you sure he doesn't want us to go straight down?"

"He made a point of wanting all of you to see the room at the same time. He hasn't been feeling well. I think he has a cold coming on. I'll go down and see what's happening."

"I'll come with you," Hinkley offered.

"I think it's better if I go alone."

Hinkley and Douglas had been partners for nearly four years. They knew each other's quirks. Hinkley was open, trusting—perhaps too much so for a police officer. Douglas was suspicious, always expecting the worst. Lately, he had been drinking heavily. Whatever had happened downstairs, whether Kevin Douglas was sick or drunk, Hinkley wanted to spare Ellen embarrassment. He was in love with her, but he kept his feelings hidden, or thought he did.

"All right. Call me if you need me."

The new rec room had a separate outside entrance. To get to it from the inside of the house you had to go through the kitchen and down the basement stairs. Ellen chose the latter. Several of the men were there helping themselves to beer from the refrigerator. She thought Kevin had put it all downstairs.

"Hope you don't mind," Jeremy Moon, a new neighbor, began. But seeing the look on Ellen Douglas's face, he set aside the can he was about to open. "What's wrong?"

"Nothing's wrong," Dave Hinkley answered for her, and gestured behind her back for Moon to drop it.

"He took a nap. Probably he's still sleeping," Ellen said. "I'll go wake him."

"Why don't we come with you?"

"No, please. I'd rather you didn't."

"Whatever you want, Ellen. We'll be right here if you need us," Moon said, and both men stepped aside.

They were in close quarters and though the other men hadn't heard the conversation, they could hardly fail to notice that something was wrong. The cheery chatter subsided to silence; the drinking stopped. Moments passed which seemed very long while they listened for some indication from below of what was going on. The tension grew till it reached a peak when Ellen called forlornly, "I can't get the door open." That galvanized them and they pounded down the stairs.

"The door's locked and he doesn't answer," she told them.

"Are you sure he's still in there?" Hinkley asked. "Maybe he went out for cigarettes or more beer, or something else?"

She shook her head. "The television's on. I can hear it."

Motioning for her to step aside with Moon, Hinkley made one more attempt to reach his partner. "Kevin! Open up!" No use, he thought, the volume was too high for him to be heard. "Have you got a key?" he asked Ellen.

"No. He was going to have one made for me, but he didn't get around to it." She sighed.

"We need to break the door down then. I'm sorry."

"Do you have to? He won't like it."

"It could be something with the gas, you know? A leak. Or if he's sick, like you say . . ."

She nodded. "Go ahead. It's only a door."

Without further discussion, the two men reared back in unison and kicked. The wood around the lock splintered and the door opened partway, still holding to its hinges. Ellen squeezed through. She didn't see her husband at first. Hinkley tried to steer her in the opposite direction so that she wouldn't be able to look directly into his face, but she broke free.

Kevin Douglas was sitting on a curved sectional of almond-colored leather that faced the mammoth TV set. The back of his head was blown out, the face imploded. He still held the gun in his right hand.

The thing Ellen Douglas wanted most in the world at that moment was to turn away from that horrid sight, but she couldn't move. Transfixed, she screamed and went on screaming.

The blaring of the TV absorbed the sound.

Hinkley took her into his arms.

TOUGH COP KILLS SELF

Holder of Record Number of Medals Blows Out Brains
Another Suicide in the Ranks

The media had shown little interest in the earlier suicides of Officers Foxworth and Kramer and more recently that of Stewart Schiff, but they couldn't ignore this or relegate it to a single column on a back page as they had done with the others.

The brass couldn't either, not in view of Kevin Douglas's record. After all, Douglas was a thirteen-year veteran.

He had made close to a thousand arrests.

He was hero of five shoot-outs.

He had been awarded the NYPD's Combat Cross three times for killing armed-robbery suspects. The Combat Cross was second in prestige only to the Medal of Honor, which is usually awarded posthumously. The word among those who were in a position to know such things was that Douglas would now receive this final tribute.

The police brass were nonplussed. A cop with that kind of record wouldn't blow his brains out without a very good reason. At least this time PC Lundy knew what attitude to take. He didn't put off a visit to the widow and immediately gave the order for a full inspector's funeral.

▼ Commissioner Lundy had the papers spread across his desk while he lectured his Chief of Detectives, Luis Deland, and his own top aide, James Felix.

"We can't make the problem go away by ignoring it. There's no way an officer with Douglas's record would commit suicide without a very good reason. We have to pray to God it's personal and not connected to this department in any way."

The two veterans on the other side of Lundy's desk nodded in unison.

"We don't need another scandal."

Again, the two chiefs nodded.

"We need to take a real close look at Douglas's personal life. Put the best people we've got on it. Use whoever you need and as many as you need. Don't scrimp. Do what you have to do."

▼ They talked about it in every precinct—in the squad rooms and in the patrol cars, in the bars where cops gathered after their shift. They even discussed it at home with their spouses.

Lieutenant Norah Mulcahaney, head of Homicide, Fourth Division, had no connection with the case but was as curious and as concerned as everybody else in the department. Things were slow that mid-June day. After two days' respite, the weather had turned bad again. Norah sat in her office on the second floor of the newly renovated station house sipping coffee and looking out the window as heavy gusts of wind turned umbrellas inside out and lashed hapless pedestrians. More rain was predicted. But if she didn't like the rain, Norah thought, neither did the crooks. During these periods the crime rate dropped appreciably.

At forty-one, Norah Mulcahaney's star was still rising. Two months ago she had taken the exam for captain, the highest rank reachable by way of civil service, and had passed with marks that put her well at the top of the list for assignment. It was rumored that she would get Manny Jacoby's job as commander of the Two-Oh when he retired for health reasons. There were only three women presently of higher rank than Lieutenant Mulcahaney in the department: an inspector and two captains. However, each captain was second in command at her respective precinct. If she got the appointment, Norah would be number one in the precinct. She looked forward to that time with confidence in her ability to perform. She believed that having overcome the inevitable jealousies and resentments accompanying her rise, she would have everyone's support.

There had been two men in Norah Mulcahaney's life; both had died violent deaths. Six years ago, Captain Joseph Capretto, her mentor and friend before he became her lover and husband, had been gunned down in the street and then run over when he tried to stop two men from raping a woman in the darkness under the Brooklyn Bridge. As the car passed over Joe, his clothing caught on the undercarriage and he was dragged for several blocks through the streets of Chinatown, before the perps realized what was happening, abandoned the car, and fled on foot.

For three years Norah didn't even think about going out with a man. She certainly didn't expect to fall in love again. Then she met Randall Tye, a journalist and television anchor. He was from another world: smart, sophisticated, at ease with celebrities, a celebrity himself. He introduced her to a new lifestyle. He wooed and won her. Then, before they were married, he too was killed. He was found on the shoulder of the Van Wyck Expressway dead of a drug overdose. Norah was devastated.

She refused to believe Randall had taken the drugs himself. She vowed there would be no third man in her life, and put all thoughts of romance out of her mind.

But she was lonely. It wasn't the kind of loneliness friends or hobbies or social activities could relieve. Norah yearned for family life. For a child. During her marriage to Joe, when it became apparent that they were not going to have a child of their own, they'd tried to adopt, but it hadn't worked out. After Randall's death, Norah tried again. As before, she applied to the Sisters of Charity.

After a couple of disappointments and heartbreaking frustration, she had at last succeeded in adopting a baby boy. He was a perfect child, with blue eyes and rosy cheeks, constantly smiling and gurgling. When Sister Beatrice, the administrator, placed him in Norah's arms, she had cried with joy and hugged him close. If only Joe and Randall had been there to share this happiness! Or her father! She decided to call the boy Patrick after her father, who had tried so hard to help with the first adoption. She invited the men and women of the Fourth Division to the baptism.

With Sister Beatrice's help, the first problem of single parenthood—finding a good reliable nanny—was solved. Colleen Kelly, who had come to New York to make her way in the world, presented herself to Sister, who sent her to Norah, who hired her on the spot.

Norah relaxed. Her joy was apparent. Her tranquillity enveloped her.

Her dark, nearly black hair was threaded with gray, but it was thick and lustrous. She wore it in a blunt cut that reached just below her chin—the square, jutting chin that was so expressive, so much an indication of Lieutenant Norah Mulcahaney's mood. Her eyes, deep blue verging on violet, were wide and alert and always inquiring. Her complexion was clear—creamy white with an underlay of rose. Lines had begun to appear; of course, at forty-one that could hardly be avoided.

The lines were particularly marked at the corners of her eyes because Norah was nearsighted and kept misplacing her glasses, forcing her to squint. And then there were the laugh lines. They had nearly disappeared, but as the routine of her life stabilized, with the job and the baby as focus, they were rapidly reappearing.

She was tall and strong. She carried herself erect and walked with an easy stride. When Norah Mulcahaney entered a room, she made her presence felt.

Heading a homicide division was not exactly a relaxing occupation, but at this time the crime rate was going down and the solution rate of the Fourth was high. There was real reason for satisfaction. But there was also reason for concern, principally with regard to the spate of alleged suicides by police officers. It disturbed Norah that while the two most recent deaths were attracting so much attention, the two earlier ones had been just about ignored. The victims had been ordinary, middle-aged, unglamorous men with average middle-class families. Norah was ashamed she couldn't even remember their names.

"Evidently, the press isn't making a connection," Norah mused aloud to Ferdi Arenas, who was sharing the coffee break.

Sergeant Arenas was ten years younger than Norah and had worked for her almost the entire length of his service in the department. He respected and admired her and didn't often disagree with any position she took.

"I hate to say this, Norah, but I think what we have here is another corruption scandal. They come up every so many years and we're just about due."

Norah shook her head.

"There are just too many similarities for these deaths to be coincidences." Ferdi warmed to his argument. "These men came from every part of the city, from different precincts, worked different jobs. There is no indication they knew each other, yet they all died in exactly the same manner. The only link I can think of is that they're involved in something illegal—drugs, prostitution, car thefts, or something brand-new we haven't even thought about yet." Ferdi threw up his hands. "I can't buy that each one killed himself in the same way for a personal, individual, unconnected motive."

The phone on Norah's desk rang.

"Homicide, Fourth Division. Lieutenant Mulcahaney. . . . Oh, hello, Chief."

In response to her silent signal, Ferdi Arenas got up and left the office, closing the door quietly and firmly behind him.

"Patrick is fine, Chief. Everything's fine. Thank you."

"Congratulations on the exam," Jim Felix went on. "You'll be getting an appointment soon."

"I'm looking forward to it, whatever it may be."

"I'm not at liberty to say, but you won't be disappointed."

Norah felt a tingle of excitement. She knew that Jim Felix hadn't called without a specific purpose. "What can I do for you, Chief?"

"You're aware, of course, of the recent rash of suicides in the ranks."

"Yes." Here it comes, she thought.

"The most recent, Detective Douglas, is shocking. He would seem to be the last person who would do away with himself. He had medals, honors, citations. . . . He was happily married, had children. As far as we know, he had no criminal connections, was not involved in anything fraudulent."

Norah gasped. She couldn't help it. Douglas had been an outstanding officer. He must have been deeply troubled to have put an end to his life. Now, instead of praising his virtues, they were probing for his vices.

"Do you know Ellen Douglas? Commissioner Lundy would like you to talk to her."

"I know her well enough to say hello—we've met at parties. But we've never really talked."

"Good enough. I want you to pay her a condolence visit. Inform her that Detective Sergeant Douglas will get an inspector's funeral. She might help in dealing with the protocol."

"Yes, sir."

"Norah . . . I'm not suggesting that you gain her confidence in order to betray it, only that you help her find out why her husband shot himself. Help her make peace with herself."

"I'll do my best."

"I know you will. The sooner the better."

A tap at her door diverted Norah's attention. She covered the mouthpiece and called, "Come." When she saw it was Ferdi, she frowned and shook her head and mouthed the words, *Not now.*

"I'm sorry. It's your housekeeper. She says it's important. Line two."

Norah's heart jumped. Had something happened to Patrick? She took her hand off the mouthpiece. "I've got a call on the other line, Jim. It's from home and it's urgent. May I call you back?"

"Go ahead. Do what you have to do and let me know if I can help."

"Thanks, Jim," She pressed the button that should have connected her to Colleen Kelly, but all she got was the dial tone.

"Ferdi!"

He came instantly.

"We were disconnected."

"No. She hung up. She said you should come straight home, but not to worry, she said, Patrick's okay."

Norah breathed a sigh of relief. She was bathed in sweat.

▼ Norah lived just across the park on East Sixty-eighth Street in the apartment she and Joe had shared. It was in a small, rent-stabilized building—one of the last such treasures in the city and it consisted of two bedrooms, each with its own bath, plus a living room and dining room—another rarity. Since there was also an eat-in kitchen, she had converted the dining room into a nursery; the second bedroom was used by the nanny. Usually, Norah walked to and from work through the park. If the weather was really bad, she took the bus. Today she didn't have the time to walk and she was too nervous to wait for the bus, so she tried to hail a cab.

After four sped by, she stepped off the curb into an overflowing gutter, practically out in the middle of the street—and was nearly run down.

"Watch where you're going! Stupid woman!" the driver snarled, but didn't slow down.

Norah watched the cab turn into the eastbound lane of the transverse and disappear.

The honking of a horn behind her warned Norah of a new danger: she was in the way of the crosstown bus. She pointed to the bus stop sign just a few feet ahead and ran for it, expecting the driver would wait for her. But he didn't pay her any attention at all, only adding insult to injury by splashing her with muddy water as he swept by.

There was not another bus in sight, not a taxi, and the nearest subway station was at Lincoln Plaza, too far away to be of use. By this time she was soaking wet and desperate. There was nothing to do but walk. It took Norah thirty-five minutes to get home. *Please God, let Colleen still be waiting.*

As she opened the front door of her apartment, Norah found her young housekeeper sitting on a straight chair in the vestibule. She was dressed for the weather in a navy pants suit, knitted cap, and rubber boots. Her luggage—two battered suitcases held together by leather straps, and assorted boxes tied with cord—was stacked beside her. Colleen Kelly wasn't crying now, but her red, swollen face indicated she had been not so long ago. And she was about to start again until she got a look at her employer.

"Ms. Mulcahaney! What's happened to you?"

"Nothing. I couldn't get a cab." Norah brushed it aside. "What's this all about? Where's Patrick?"

"In bed. Sleeping."

"Thank God!" Norah took a moment to calm down. "You scared the life out of me, Colleen." She indicated the luggage. "What's all this? Where are you going?"

"Newfoundland," the girl replied promptly.

"What?"

"Newfoundland. That's where the plane went down. There's been a terrible accident, Ms. Norah. The plane exploded in midair. They don't know who the survivors are, if there are any. Mum and Dad were supposed to be on that flight. I have to go in case . . . to identify . . ." She started to sob.

"Slow down, Colleen. Let's go and sit down together." Norah tried to lead the distraught girl to the living room, but Colleen shook her off.

Pink-cheeked and plump, with raven hair, Colleen moved in quick little jerky steps that reminded Norah of a pouter pigeon. "I can't. The car will be here any minute to pick me up and take me to the airport. They're flying the families to the site to identify . . . Oh poor Mum, poor Dad . . ."

Norah hadn't listened to the radio all day, but she was able to put Colleen's broken phrases together. Apparently, there had been a midair explosion and her parents had been passengers on the flight.

"I didn't know they were coming over. You said they might, but I had no idea they'd decided or that the visit was imminent."

"Nor I, Ms. Norah, nor I. My Aunt Bridget in Dublin, she called to inform me, to spare me the shock of hearing it from a stranger or over the radio," the young woman moaned. "They won the tickets in a raffle, Aunt Bridget said. Oh, they were so happy and excited to be coming!" Colleen wailed, and fished for a tissue from her handbag. "I'm sorry to be leaving you like this without any notice, Ms. Norah. And to leave the boy. But you'll have no trouble getting someone to look after him. He's so good. You won't have any trouble."

"Of course not. You mustn't worry about it. Anyway, you'll be back before we know it. Your mum and dad are going to be fine and you'll all be back before we know it."

Further assurances were cut short by the buzzer downstairs.

"It's here! The car's here!" Colleen cried out. While she tried frantically to lift the suitcases and the boxes all at once, Norah buzzed the driver in. In great confusion the three of them managed to jam themselves and Colleen's possessions into the tiny self-service elevator. It occurred to Norah as she watched Colleen's things being loaded that the nanny had packed just about everything she owned. It wasn't a good omen.

"Call me and let me know what's happened. Be sure to call if you need anything," Norah said, and hugged the girl. "You'll be back before we know it."

Waving goodbye, Norah caught a glimpse of the other passengers, relatives—she supposed—of others on the catastrophic flight. They looked to be in shock, all of them. She murmured a short prayer that God in His mercy might spare those they loved.

Back in the house, Norah locked and bolted the front door, and then went down the hall to Patrick's room to look in on him. He was sleeping peacefully, breathing lightly. The sight brought a smile to Norah's face. As she stood watching her son, Patrick stirred in his sleep. His brow furrowed, then cleared as he smiled. He was a happy child and she a happy woman. Suddenly, she remembered she was supposed to call Jim Felix. According to her watch, he had probably left already, but she had to give it a try.

▼ "We've been waiting for your call." Paula Lawson managed to make it a reprimand. "Please hold."

Norah expected to be kept on hold for a while as penance, and was surprised to be put through right away.

Felix was all concern. "Is everything all right? Is the boy okay?"

"Yes, thank God. It's the nanny. Her mother and father were on that World-Air plane that exploded this morning."

"God!"

"She got a call from the airline offering to fly her to the scene. She doesn't know what she'll find when she gets there."

"That's terrible. Is there anything I can do?"

"I wish there were. The thing is, I can't leave Patrick till I get a substitute nanny. I'll make a few calls, but I don't think I can get to that visit with Ellen Douglas anytime soon."

"Of course not. I understand. There's no urgency. Take all the time you need."

CHAPTER 3

▼ Neither Chief Felix nor Norah herself had anticipated the difficulties. There were six names on Norah's list of acceptable substitute baby-sitters, but none was available on a regular basis or for an extended period of time. This one could give her Thursdays and Fridays, nine to five. That one Mondays, five till midnight. Some could only manage a few hours and couldn't guarantee the same day every week. It would mean a stream of strangers that would confuse Patrick. It would mean her running back and forth from the precinct, working with one eye on the clock and worrying about what was going on at home.

First thing in the morning, she called Captain Manny Jacoby to explain her situation and to advise him that she wouldn't be in till noon. She'd arranged for Ferdi Arenas to cover the chart—that is, to make the daily assignments and to stand in for her when necessary. Finally, she contacted Jim Felix to suggest he assign someone else to interview Ellen Douglas. He said he'd wait till she was available.

That done, Norah settled down to a methodical phone canvass of the home-care agencies. The urgency of her need dismayed them. They were not prepared to deal with it. One or two did rally and promised they would round up candidates for her to interview. Meanwhile, Patrick still had to be cared for. He was no longer a babe in arms, having grown into a sturdy toddler, big for his age. He walked with assurance and his vocabulary was expanding rapidly. Nevertheless, he had to be bathed and fed. These were chores in which Norah delighted. Tending the child, holding him and feeling his warmth, was unalloyed joy. Norah had never been so happy.

After lunch, she called Manny Jacoby to say she wasn't going to make it to work after all. She might even have to take some days off. A week maybe.

Jacoby was not as understanding as he had been earlier. "When do you think you'll find somebody?"

"How can I answer that, Captain? I've called every home- and child-care agency in the five boroughs. I've already interviewed half a dozen women. Some of them are qualified in a professional sense but have no warmth or love in them. Others have plenty of love to give but can't make a bed or prepare a meal for a child. Also, I need to know something about the individual's background. I can't just let anyone into my house and leave him alone with my child."

Manny Jacoby sighed aggrievedly.

"Things are slow right now," Norah reasoned. "Sergeant Arenas can cover the chart and fill in for me generally. If there's a problem, he can call me. It's not like I was going somewhere you couldn't reach me. I'll be right here at the end of the telephone."

There was a long silence at the other end. Jacoby was not a well man. Paunchy and balding, he was troubled by severe arthritis. At forty-six, young by today's standards, he had suffered a heart attack and now wore a pacemaker. He was an administrator by choice, known to be conservative, to "go by the book." So he was spared from the danger and stress of the streets. He feared that one day he would be forced to emerge from the sanctuary of the precinct house. How would his heart respond?

What he needed was a second-in-command. Someone not too young, but mature. Capable. Dedicated. Ambitious, in the sense of wanting to make a contribution, but not after his job. He wanted Norah Mulcahaney. Norah had passed the captain's exam with flying colors, as she had all previous tests, and she expected to be given a precinct command as her next assignment. Everyone expected it. Upon such a promotion it was customary to move the officer to another venue so that he or she could start with a clean slate. Jacoby intended to apply to the C of D to make an exception and give Norah to him. Norah and he could work together. Hadn't they already proved it?

When Norah Mulcahaney had first come to Homicide and the Two-Oh, the only question in Manny Jacoby's mind had been: How long will she last? She'd lasted long enough to gain his respect and that of the men and women who worked with her, to make lieutenant and now captain. The new responsibilities and the different problems she encountered honed her skills. They strengthened and changed her. Inevitably, they toughened her. But since the adoption, she had changed again. She was, Jacoby thought, trying to analyze it . . . gentler, more feminine. The Job didn't come first anymore.

"Are you really sure you want to find somebody?" he asked.

The question shocked Norah.

"You could put Patrick in day care, you know. Maybe with the nuns where you got him. Temporarily, of course."

"Never!" Norah flamed scarlet. Two years into their marriage Norah and Joe had adopted a three-year-old, Mark. Their happiness didn't last. After only a few months a woman, the mistress of a notorious mafioso, revealed herself and claimed to be the boy's natural mother. She didn't want the boy back. No, the threat was not that simple. Joe Capretto had certain evidence that would convict her lover. Unless he turned it over, she would reveal herself to Mark. Whether Joe gave in to her demand or not, the possibility of further demands would hang over the three of them for the rest of their lives. For all their sakes, there was nothing to do but relinquish the child.

The pain would always be there, deep inside Norah. The memory of the hurt in the boy's eyes as she handed him over to the nun would never go away. Many a night Norah's pillow was stained by her tears. She wondered if Mark ever thought of her. If he remembered.

Probably not. And it was best for it to be wiped away as most childhood memories are. She prayed that he had forgotten her in the loving care of another mother and another family. And if God ever saw fit to bless her with a child again, she vowed to never let him leave her.

"I'll never send Patrick back! Not for one day, not for an hour. I'll resign first."

"Who said anything about resigning?" Jacoby blustered. "Take it easy. Take all the time you need to find the right person. I don't want you coming back with any worries over Patrick. I want you with a clear mind. Meantime, you can catch up with the paperwork. Right?"

That was more like the Manny Jacoby she knew, Norah thought, and smiled.

"How about Joe's sisters? Couldn't one of them . . ."

There were seven girls in Joe's family. One had died skydiving. Three were married with families of their own. Three lived in Los Angeles and had careers of their own.

"No, sir, and I wouldn't put them in the position of having to turn me down. A couple of the agencies I've contacted have responded with some good prospects. I'm optimistic," she assured Captain Jacoby.

▼ As the hours passed, Norah's optimism faded. She grew more and more discouraged. She arranged for one of the women she was accustomed to using on a part-time basis to come in and watch Patrick while she paid a visit to the squad to make sure everything was running smoothly under Ferdi Arenas's supervision. But even in that short time she was distracted, constantly looking at her watch. Patrick had to be bathed, put into his pajamas, and given his dinner. The woman who was with him now was not accustomed to doing all that.

"Everything looks good, Ferdi. Very good. If there's any problem, any question, just call me." Tomorrow she'd have to do some marketing and then there was laundry . . .

Ferdi was aware of her preoccupation. No use trying to talk to her now, he thought, and walked her to the door. "Good luck, Lieutenant."

She could hire a good cleaning service, but she'd have to be present while they worked.

"Good luck," Ferdi murmured to himself.

▼ For the next two days nobody from the squad even called. Norah appreciated being left alone. Well into the third day, she began to worry. Were they getting along that well without her? She broke first.

"Ferdi? It's Norah. How are you doing over there?"

"Fine. We're okay. How about you? Have you found a nanny?"

"I've got a couple of strong possibilities. I'm checking them out." That wasn't true. So far she'd found no one she would even consider trusting with Patrick.

"I hope one of them works out. We sure miss you. We've got two new cases—both juvenile homicides. You've read about them?"

"Haven't had the time." Norah was ashamed to admit she was so absorbed in Patrick that she hadn't had the interest even to read the newspapers or turn on the news.

"One is the allegedly accidental shooting of a twelve-year-old kid by his eight-year-old brother. The other's a drive-by. The perp is fifteen. The DA wants to try him as an adult and charge manslaughter. I'm not sure the evidence will support it."

Norah frowned. "Why didn't you tell me? You should have called."

"I tried to tell you when you were here, but you didn't seem interested. Anyway, Captain Jacoby said to leave you alone and not bother you."

"Captain Jacoby wants to spare me any distraction, but I want to know what's going on. In the future, call and tell me, please." She had no intention of intruding in either case; it was a matter of policy, of establishing a precedent. "Meantime, I want to see the DD5's on both cases. Have somebody drop them off."

"Sure." Arenas was obviously relieved. "What about Captain Jacoby?"

"I'll make it right with him," Norah promised.

In no time the phone started to ring again, if not with the frequency it did at the squad, then often enough to make Norah feel she was back in the flow and to make her blood race. The downstairs buzzer heralded the arrival of messengers that shuttled back and forth across the park. Each night, Ferdi dropped by on his way home to give her a rundown of the day's events and to discuss the next day's assignments. It was like the real thing. Except she missed the freedom to get out and interview witnesses herself.

CHAPTER 4

▼ Carol Ciccerone MacKenzie was late coming home. She had stayed after school to tutor a student and then stopped to pick up a few things at the supermarket. Passing the bakery, she decided to splurge on a luscious-looking Black Forest cake, a family favorite. It was to celebrate her being offered a full-time job. Carol MacKenzie taught history at a parochial school in Manhattan, but she was only a substitute. Today, the principal had called her in and asked if she would be willing to work full-time.

Carol could hardly contain herself, but managed, she hoped, not to sound too eager. "Yes," she replied, having waited as long as she dared.

Could she manage in view of the fact that her own two girls attended another school? Sister Rose wanted to know.

No problem, Carol had hastened to assure her. Her father was retired and living with them. He was already accompanying the girls to school in the morning and picking them up in the afternoon. He would continue to do so till there was an opening for them here.

She would try to expedite that, the principal assured Carol, and they exchanged smiles of satisfaction.

How soon could she start?

Right now, Carol had replied. And they had shaken hands on it.

Carol was still bathed in the glow of the interview when she turned the corner of her block. She only had to drive around once more before she found a parking place on the other side of the street. Things were going her way at last, she exulted. She expertly backed her ancient Volkswagen into the open space, cut the motor, and got out. Collecting the groceries, the bakery box, and the briefcase in which she carried her school papers, she crossed the street and walked up to her front porch, where she put everything down so she could fish her keys out of her purse. She selected the one she wanted but was surprised, when she put it in the lock, that the door was already open. Not uneasy—the girls were careless sometimes—but wary, she entered. Everything seemed all right.

"I'm home," she sang out, heading down a long, narrow corridor to the kitchen in the rear.

There was no answer. Putting her bundles down on the kitchen table, she returned to the front hall and stood at the bottom of the stairs. "Dad? Where are you?"

The girls attended a private school. It was expensive, a hardship for Carol and her father, but both considered it a necessity, not a luxury or an affectation. The Sacred Heart Academy, a school for girls, provided excellent instruction and strong security. It had the best record for safety in all of the five boroughs. Its students were least likely to be carrying guns or using drugs. It was a shame that that should be a consideration in selecting a school, Carol and her father agreed, but that was the world they lived in.

"Dad! Are you upstairs?" This time there was anxiety in Carol's voice.

On a fine day it was not unusual for her father to call for his granddaughters at the school and take them through the park on the way home. Sometimes they strolled through the zoo; the girls loved to watch the seals. They might stop in at one of the museums, but this was no day for it. In any event, they were always back by five, and it was already well past that.

"Dad!" she cried out, impelled by a sudden, nameless fear as she bounded up the stairs to her father's room.

The one-family house stood at the end of a row of assorted-style houses on a quiet, residential street on the Upper West Side. Once Carol MacKenzie's only asset, the house had become a liability. Her husband, Howard, had inherited it from his father, who inherited it from his. The first Howard built it. A canny Scot, he had amassed a modest fortune which was slowly consumed over the years by his progeny. The money wasn't squandered, but lost through bad investments. By the time Carol and her Howard married and moved in, the house was heavily mortgaged. By careful management of Howard's salary, which fluctuated unpredictably—he was a salesman of kitchen supplies for restaurants, who worked on commission—they were able to continue to live there. They and their two girls were happy.

Without warning, their lives were shattered. Returning from a sales convention in Philadelphia, Howard MacKenzie swerved to avoid a light van changing lanes and hit another car that came up on his left. The air bag deployed and broke his neck, killing him instantly.

There was no pension, no death benefits. Carol couldn't go back to work without someone to look after the girls. Her parents gave up their apartment and moved in with her. They had barely adjusted to the arrangement when a freak fire took the life of Amelia Ciccerone.

Upon the death of his wife of thirty-one years, Sergeant William Ciccerone put in for retirement. He would stay home to look after the girls. With Carol's paycheck and his pension, they could just about make it. But taxes kept going up, as did utilities and heating oil. After a while their combined incomes were not sufficient. Where could they cut down? Not on the girls' school; that was out of the question. Carol and her father talked about selling the house and moving. But where would they go? Though the house was in a sad state of disrepair both inside and out, they couldn't duplicate what it provided.

The house was just large enough to suit everyone. Carol had the master bedroom, of course. The girls shared a small room on the second floor. Bill Ciccerone converted the room he'd occupied with his wife into a combination den and office. It was intended not only to provide him with a private place but also to exorcise the ghost of Amelia. He removed the queen-sized bed that had occupied the center of the room and replaced it with a narrow cot in one corner. That made space for a plain but serviceable desk and an orthopedic swivel chair, both rescued from recent precinct house renovations. A file cabinet was stuffed with reports of old cases he had worked. Bookcases covered the walls from floor to ceiling and were filled to overflowing. What didn't fit was stacked in neat piles on the floor. The old books in their various bindings, commendations earned over the years, group photographs of old buddies, all combined to give Ciccerone's retreat warmth and dignity. Only a personal computer in its gleaming newness indicated that the retired policeman did not live exclusively in the past.

It was her father's sanctuary, and even in a moment of desperate anxiety, Carol hesitated to intrude. She knocked lightly.

"Dad?" Not getting a reply this time either, she opened the door cautiously and stood transfixed by what she saw.

Bill Ciccerone was slumped in his special chair at his old desk, the same desk where he had sat for twenty-two of his thirty years of service. His head was thrown back and slightly to the right. Blood and bone were everywhere. His thinning hair was matted with it. His right hand hung loose over the arm of the chair. It held a gun.

"Dad!" Carol cried out. "Oh, Daddy!" Raising her eyes slowly, she dared to look at her father's face. One look and then she fled.

She barely made it to the hall bathroom, where she heaved her entire lunch. It took a while for her to recover enough to call 911. Response time was seven and a half minutes, but it was too late. It had already been too late when she made the call.

▼ The 911 call was routinely routed to Homicide, Fourth Division, and Danny Neel caught the squeal.

Detective Danny Neel came from three generations of cops. His grandfather had been a sergeant, his father a full inspector; he expected to surpass them both. He had one problem: he was too quick and too expert with his fists. Therefore he was too ready to rely on them. That kind of policing was out of style and had been for some time. Neel knew it and tried to channel his instincts by boxing on the police team, middleweight division. In his late twenties, he had dark curly hair, dark eyes, and very white skin. He had a fine set of teeth which he liked to show off, along with a dimple at the right, by smiling often. He was single and lived at home, but there was a girlfriend. There was always a girlfriend.

By the time Detective Neel arrived at the scene it was well after six, but sunset was still a good hour and a half away.

It was your typical big-city crime scene. Sawhorses had been placed at each end of the block to seal it. RMPs were lined up in front of the Ciccerone house, their roof lights revolving, constantly sweeping the crowds of neighbors who came out to watch. Neel pulled up in his 4×4 and showed his ID. An opening was made in the barricades so he could drive through. He was met by a uniform from the Two-Oh whom he recognized but whose name he couldn't remember. He squinted at the nameplate. "What've we got here, Officer . . . Wren?"

"The victim is Sergeant Ciccerone," Wren replied, and waited for the reaction. "Bill Ciccerone? Desk sergeant at the Two-Oh and recently retired? You remember him? Everybody knew old Bill."

Officer Robert Wren, red-faced and corpulent, wasn't so young himself. He took a much-used handkerchief out of his back pocket and wiped his face, which immediately brought up a new surge of sweat. "Killed himself like the others. Blew out his brains just like they did—single shot in the mouth. Who would have believed it!"

Neel tensed right away. "Is that what the ME says?"

"No sir, he hasn't got here yet, but you don't need an ME for this one, Detective. Take a look for yourself—upstairs, first door to the left."

Neel intended to do just that—in due course. "Nine-one-one says the daughter called it in. I'll talk to her first. Where is she?"

Officer Wren was clearly upset. "She wasn't here when we rang the bell. The door was unlocked, so we just walked in. There was nobody here. The house was empty, except for the victim."

Danny Neel pursed his lips thoughtfully. Looked like he'd been handed a can of worms. Not that he avoided the tough cases—how could you make a reputation if you took on only the open-and-shut cases? He welcomed the *mysteries,* which was how the tough ones were known in police parlance, but this one was layers upon layers. Danny leaned on the theory that Ciccerone's death was a suicide and was connected to the other recent suicides of police officers, but he couldn't imagine how. He'd heard rumors that the PC and even the mayor were taking an interest. That kind of pressure he didn't need.

Now there was this added twist of the daughter's disappearance.

Why would she call 911 and then run away? Maybe the trauma of finding her father dead, his brains oozing from his head, had been too much for her and she'd done what instinct told her to do—flee. So he'd better get up there and see precisely what they were confronting.

It was pretty bad, Neel acknowledged as he stood on the threshold of Ciccerone's study. He had to work himself up to going inside to take a closer look. Oh yes, he remembered old Bill, but if he hadn't already known who it was, he wouldn't have recognized him. The impact on someone who cared for him would have been almost beyond bearing.

He shifted his attention to the gun in the dead officer's hand. It was standard police-issue, probably old Bill's service revolver. *God! What a way to go.* It took some kind of anguish to make you put the barrel of a gun into your mouth and pull the trigger. He couldn't do it, Neel thought.

There had been a lull in the activity downstairs, but now Danny heard a car pull up. He went to the window and recognized the assistant ME's black Buick. Then close behind he heard the bleep of the morgue wagon. No need for him to stand around while the ME examined the body, when even a uniform was able to determine the cause of death and connect it to the previous cop suicides. But the situation did require his reporting to a superior. At the moment, that was Sergeant Fernando Arenas.

He shouldn't delay, Danny reminded himself.

When he got Neel's call, Ferdi did some soul-searching of his own.

He decided he couldn't risk waiting the hour or so until he would routinely be visiting Norah Mulcahaney. As head of the squad she should be either notified immediately or passed over entirely. That would mean contacting Captain Jacoby.

The more Ferdi thought about it, the more he became convinced that there was no need to go over Norah's head, that in fact, it would be wrong to do so.

▼ Upon getting Ferdi's call, Norah's adrenaline began to flow. She remembered Bill Ciccerone. How many years had he manned the desk at the Two-Oh? How many times during those years had she passed him on the way upstairs to the squad? Never had Ciccerone failed to give her a friendly greeting, never wavering whether she was riding high or in trouble. He had showed support in time of personal loss or professional trouble.

Norah was well aware of his personal history. She knew he had a married daughter, Carol, with two children, who had lived around the corner from him and his wife. She knew that Carol's husband had been killed and Carol had had trouble collecting the insurance because the insurance company charged that Howard had been DWI. The case went to court and the company won. It was an emotional as well as an economic blow. With the family's primary source of income gone, Carol had had to go back to work and her parents had moved in with her. When Amelia Ciccerone died, Sergeant Ciccerone had decided to retire.

He wasn't ready to retire. Norah recalled the tears in his eyes at the party they'd given for him. Recent reports from friends who had visited Bill indicated that he was adjusting to his new role and was very much aware of his responsibilities with regard to the girls. He was teaching them how to skate, first on Rollerblades and then on ice. He took them to museums, attended all school functions, especially when their mother could not. All in all, he was a good and caring grandfather.

What could have happened to drive him to such despair?

Everything Ferdi had told her so far only increased Norah's desire to see for herself. It wasn't possible. She couldn't get away.

"What does Carol say about her father's mood? Was he depressed over their financial situation?"

"Neel didn't talk to the daughter. She wasn't there. Nobody was there," Arenas replied.

"Hold on a minute. I thought she was the one, Carol MacKenzie, who notified nine-one-one."

"A woman called and gave that name, but according to the RMPs at the scene, the house was empty when they got there."

Norah frowned. "How about the children? Were they there?"

"To tell you the truth, Lieutenant, I don't know. Detective Neel wasn't specific when he notified me."

At that moment, Norah was not concerned with Danny Neel's performance. She was considering whether she could somehow make time to go over to this latest scene of a police officer's death and assess the situation herself. She looked at her watch: six-thirty. Today's sitter would be leaving at eight. Maybe she could be persuaded to stay a while longer.

"Hang on for a couple of minutes," she told Ferdi, and went to the nursery.

Fiona Quinn, another in the seemingly endless stream of young

Irishwomen who like Colleen Kelly came to New York to find their fortunes, had given Patrick his bath, dried and dusted him. She had him in his pajamas and was putting him to bed when Norah came in. As soon as he saw her, the boy held out chubby arms.

"Mama, Mama . . ."

She held him close, feeling his warmth, and her heart pounded with happiness. She kissed the crown of his blond head.

"I was just coming to look for you, Lieutenant," Fiona Quinn said. "I need to ask you a favor. Do you mind if I leave a bit early? Patrick's had his supper and his bath, so he's all set. If you wouldn't mind . . ."

Norah interrupted. "I was just going to ask you if you wouldn't mind staying a few extra hours."

"Oh gosh! I'm so sorry, Lieutenant, but I've got this real big date. His name's Jerry and he plays guitar with the Hot Rocks. I worked real hard to get him to ask me out. If I stand him up, I may never get another chance."

"How about if I double the fee?"

Fiona hesitated, and for a moment Norah thought money had triumphed.

"I'm real sorry, Lieutenant." Fiona Quinn backed away a couple of steps. "Call me when you need me again," she sputtered, then turned and fled.

Norah returned to the telephone.

"The sitter can't stay," she told Ferdi. "I'll try a couple of others, but I don't have much hope. It's only Monday. You'd think it was Saturday night," she muttered.

"What about me?" Ferdi asked. "I'm available. As the father of two, I know my way around a nursery. And I work cheap."

"You?"

"Why not? I can watch the ball game on your TV same as on mine."

Norah was sorely tempted. "Aren't you on duty?"

"No, ma'am. If I go to the scene now, I'll be on overtime."

The department in general and Captain Jacoby in particular were on a big drive to cut down on overtime. Norah, on the other hand, was very liberal about it, an attitude for which she was frequently criticized.

"What about Concepción?" That was Ferdi's wife. "Won't she mind?"

"Concepción expected I'd be working late, so she took the children over to her mother's. They'll all stay overnight."

Norah made no protests. "Thanks, Ferdi." She hung up.

Though sunset was not till sometime after eight P.M., the sky was already dark and it seemed the rain would be returning sooner than predicted. So Norah put on her raincoat—the one she wore in all but the worst snowstorms—and boots that came up to her ankles. She was eager, more excited than she could remember being about a case in a long time. It would be good to get out of the house. She put that thought aside quickly.

Basically, Norah was an investigator. She needed to be involved, to make personal contact with witnesses and suspects. The higher one rose in rank, the more removed from actual policing one became. Norah was an excellent administrator, but her heart wasn't in it, and that was why she would never rise higher than captain. And she didn't care.

She was dressed and ready, waiting beside the front door, when Ferdi Arenas arrived. She motioned for him to follow her to Patrick's room.

The boy was sleeping lightly. Sensing their presence, he opened his eyes wide. "Mama," he murmured, and smiled a sleepy smile.

She bent over him and kissed him. "You remember Uncle Ferdi? I have to go out tonight, but he'll be here in the house with you till I get back. Okay? If you need anything, you know what to do."

The child nodded, blue eyes solemn as he pointed to the remote beside his bed. "Push the red button and speak."

"Good," Norah praised. She had had a monitoring system installed that made it possible to supervise Patrick from her bedroom, the nanny's room, and the living room. "So you can watch the game at ease," she told Ferdi.

▼ The ME, Phillip Worgan, answered the call himself, an indication of how concerned the brass were. But by the time Norah arrived at the scene of Bill Ciccerone's death, Worgan had come and gone; the body was waiting to be transported to the morgue, where a full autopsy would be conducted ASAP. The bulk of the police presence had been cleaned out and only members of the forensic crime scene squad were still there. They were painstakingly collecting the scraps of evidence which had become the foundation of modern crime detection: one expert had pronounced that DNA evidence carried more weight with a jury today than an eyewitness account.

"What've you got?" Norah asked Danny Neel.

In a few terse sentences the young detective with the toothy smile described the situation as he had found it upon his arrival, and then what he'd found upstairs.

She studied him. "I'd better see for myself."

It was not Danny Neel's place to try to dissuade her. He merely nodded and led her up the stairs to the second floor, stopping at the first door on the left. He opened it for her and stepped aside.

Norah caught her breath and for several moments remained transfixed. The poor man, she thought, and quickly looked away.

Her first impression was of disorder. Books everywhere. She observed the custom-crafted bookcases which had been installed along an entire wall and were filled to overflowing. The books, magazines, and pamphlets in piles on the floor, the photographs standing in ranks on every available surface. Faded by time, the faces were barely recognizable. Norah examined them closely, even putting on her glasses to do it. Mostly they were pictures of groups and organizations to which Bill Ciccerone had belonged and in which he took pride and pleasure. His high school graduation class, his official Police Academy graduation photograph. His wedding photo was there, as well as a shot of the NYPD Softball Team of 1994, with Norah herself in a row of spectators! Nothing later than that was displayed; nothing useful that she could see. So, she thought, this sad jumble composed the old cop's life. This is what's left.

She moved on to the orthopedic chair Ciccerone had used for so many years. She noted shape and location of the bloodstains on the chair and the desk and across an open travel brochure. The destination was Hawaii.

"He was sitting there when he was discovered," Danny Neel said before he was asked. "His head was tilted back and toward the right shoulder. The gun was in his lap, his finger still curled around the trigger. The back of his head . . ." He paused.

"I know. Did anyone find the bullet?"

"Nobody looked, as far as I know."

Norah sighed heavily. "Did Worgan give a cause of death?"

"I didn't ask. It was obvious. I thought . . . I'm sorry."

"What did Worgan say? Did he say the wound was self-inflicted?"

Norah fixed her "serious" look on him.

Neel swallowed, took his notebook from the inside pocket of his jacket, leafed through it to the right page, and read. "Doc Worgan said '*apparently* self-inflicted.' "

"How about time of death?"

Neel turned to the next page. "Between twelve and two P.M."

"The girls would have been at school," Norah reasoned aloud. "What time was the nine-one-one call logged?"

"Just short of five P.M.—four forty-nine."

"School usually lets out around three, I think."

"I'll find out."

"It's possible she got home at her regular time but didn't go up to her father's room and didn't know what had happened. Anyway, she did find him ultimately, made the call, and then walked away. Why?"

Neel said nothing. He watched Norah and waited. This was the lieut at her best.

"Why didn't she stay home and wait for the police?" Norah continued developing the idea. "Because the children weren't home and they should have been! I think we can assume that the children were not permitted to come home by themselves—not in this city, at this time, at their age. I remember Bill Ciccerone complaining about the cost of the school. For what they charged they should pick up and deliver door to door, he'd said. One of the principal reasons he was retiring was to look after his girls, including but not limited to getting them back and forth from school. Apparently on this day he was derelict. Let's assume, therefore, Carol MacKenzie came home to find her father slumped at his desk, the back of his head blown away and the gun still in his hand . . . and the girls missing. What would she do? What would any mother have done?"

"Call nine-one-one," Danny answered promptly.

"No! She'd call the school. Both private and parochial schools arc very careful not to let students go off with any strangers. I'll give you odds that the MacKenzie girls were there waiting for someone to come and get them."

"Makes sense, Loo." Danny Neel flashed his famous smile. "But where are they now?"

Once again Norah looked around the confines in which a man had lived and died. The heavy odor of blood tainted the entire house.

"She didn't bring them back here, obviously. We need to find them. But that shouldn't be too difficult. Somebody in the neighborhood is sure to know what school the girls attend or where Mrs. MacKenzie works."

While she spoke, Danny Neel's attention wandered. "Hey, Lieutenant, look!" He pointed to the window in back of Norah. "Could that be her coming up the walk?"

CHAPTER 5

▼ Norah and Danny went downstairs to meet Carol MacKenzie as she entered her home. She gasped when she saw them standing side by side in the darkening vestibule.

"Mrs. MacKenzie? Don't be frightened. We're police. I'm Lieutenant Mulcahaney and this is Detective Neel."

Both displayed their ID wallets.

The color drained from Carol MacKenzie's face. She swayed. Both Norah and Danny jumped to catch her. Half dragging and half carrying, they managed to get her into the parlor and put her on the nearest couch.

"Are you all right? Can we get you anything? A glass of water?" Norah asked.

"Thank you. A glass of water. The kitchen is . . ."

"I'll find it," Danny assured her, and left.

Norah waited till he was back with the water and the young mother took the glass with a hand that shook and set it aside after only a couple of sips.

"I came to get some things for overnight for the girls and myself. I thought that by now everyone would be gone."

"Then I should warn you that there are still some detectives upstairs. Your father had many friends. He was well liked at the precinct. We want to make sure that we know exactly what happened and why. The why is very important, Mrs. MacKenzie."

"I can't believe he did this. I can't believe it." Fumbling in her handbag, Carol brought out an already soggy ball of tissue and began to cry into it. Norah and Danny exchanged glances.

"Why did you leave the house after reporting what had happened to your father?" Norah was careful to be gentle. It was almost like dealing with a small, frightened animal. "Why did you wait to come back till you thought the police would be gone?"

"I just couldn't deal with all the questions. I couldn't cope."

"You've been interrogated by the police before?"

"My husband died in an auto accident just about two years ago. He was driving home from a sales convention in Philadelphia. On the Pulaski Skyway, he collided with a car changing lanes. The driver of the other car survived and claimed Howard was driving like a madman, that he was driving while *impaired.* That's a polite word for drunk. Well, let me tell you, I know there's a lot of drinking goes on at these affairs, but Howard was never drunk in his life. Never. He might, when entertaining an important customer, have a beer. Two was his limit. They tried to shake me, but they couldn't. Dad had to come down and set them straight."

"Was there a blood test?" Norah asked.

"No."

There should have been, Norah thought. They might have thought the case was open-and-shut and no test was necessary.

"Of course, when they found out who my dad was, they were ever so sorry. They apologized, but what good was it?"

"That was a bad experience, certainly, but not all police harass a witness in that manner." Norah tried to reassure her.

"A year later, almost to the day, my mother passed on. It was a freak accident. By then my parents were living with me and the girls. The heat in the house was off because Con Ed was working in the street. My mother felt the chill and brought out the kerosene heater and put it near her chair. She fell asleep reading. Somehow the heater must have tipped over and caught the edge of a blanket, causing a small fire that was quickly put out. But my mother had a weak heart and she died of smoke inhalation."

"I'm sorry," Norah murmured, and Neel, standing apart, made sounds of sympathy.

"The insurance company turned down our claims. Their investigators reported the fire was caused by my mother's negligence and so we were not entitled to be reimbursed for the damage. My mother's life was not insured. We couldn't afford it."

"I'm very sorry."

"They pried into every crevice of our lives to make my mother out to be irresponsible. They found out she'd had a couple of similar accidents when she and my father had their own place. In each instance the damage had been so slight that my dad didn't even put in a claim. They made that sound sinister, as though he had some ulterior motive." Carol MacKenzie paused. "You don't know what it's like to have your motives impugned, every word you speak turned against you."

"I understand."

"No, you don't. The lawyers presented my mother as more than careless—unbalanced was the word they used. They said she had dementia! She was old and she was forgetful; that's a crime these days, I suppose."

"I understand that when you came home this afternoon and discovered your father's body you anticipated what the police would do and say and you couldn't deal with it." Norah's tone and her look were full of compassion.

"I can take it, Lieutenant. I've been taking it for a few years now. Believe me, there's no situation I haven't faced, no accusation or insinuation I haven't parried. It's my girls I'm worried about. I helped them to cope with the death of their father, and after that— their grandma. How am I going to explain that their grandpa is gone too? How can I bring them back into this house?"

"You'll have to sooner or later."

"How can I tell them that he took his own life?"

"You'll have to and you will. God will give you the strength. Where were you planning to spend the night?"

"The principal of the school where I teach has offered us a room in the convent for as long as we need it. So, please, I'd like to get what I came for and leave."

"Of course. I have just a few questions."

"Haven't you understood anything I've said?" Carol MacKenzie's temper flared. Tears sprang into her tired eyes and coursed down her haggard cheeks. "My dad has left me alone with two fatherless children to bring up and no money. All I have is this albatross of a house. What am I going to do? How am I going to cope?" She was beginning to shake. "How could he abandon us like this! How could he do it?"

Norah waited till she got herself in hand. "I was going to ask you the same thing."

That stopped the incipient hysterics like a stinging slap.

"Let me see if I've got this right," Norah resumed quietly. "This house belonged to your husband, Howard MacKenzie, who had inherited it from his father. When he died in an auto accident, it devolved on you. In order to meet expenses, your parents moved in to keep house for you and to look after the girls. Then there was the fire and your mother died. That left you with the problem of the girls. Neither you nor your father could stay home from work and there was no money to hire someone to do it for you. The problem was solved by your father's early retirement. He readily admitted that his main reason for retiring was to help you and to look after his grandchildren. Between his pension and your earnings, you could just about make out. Right?"

"Right."

"It was working out then. Everybody was happy. What went wrong?"

"Nothing. Nothing went wrong."

"Then why did your father kill himself?" Norah persisted. "You father loved his grandkids—that's how he referred to them—and he was prepared to make any sacrifice for their sake. From the papers I saw in his room, it appears he was getting material together for a book. Memoirs are very popular right now, and I'm sure Sergeant Ciccerone had many stories to tell." Norah took a breath. "It seems to me these are preparations for the future, not for death. We can't let it go like that, Mrs. MacKenzie."

"He had a heart condition over many years. He took medicine for it."

Norah shook her head. "I don't see that as sufficient motivation . . . unless it took a sudden turn for the worse. Had he seen his doctor lately?"

"Yes. He went in for a routine checkup a couple of weeks ago. I asked him how it went and he said all was well. The tests were fine and the doctor said to continue what he was doing." She paused, shuddering. "But suppose everything wasn't fine? Suppose something really bad had shown up and he didn't want to worry me?"

"It's a possibility, of course," Norah admitted. "But to choose to die is one thing, to choose to die in such a violent manner . . ." She shook her head slowly. "I'll speak to his doctors of course, but meantime I'd like you to think very hard about the last weeks and the last days. Was there any drastic change in your father's moods? Was he depressed? Was there any change in his daily routine?"

"He was a little down, but I didn't relate it to the medical checkup. He had a bad cold. Actually, as it developed it was more like the flu with fever, chills, severe coughing. He'd planned to take the girls to the Museum of Natural History on Saturday to see the dinosaur exhibit but he had to postpone it. They were very disappointed, but it was plain Dad didn't really feel well at all. He stayed in his room all weekend. He even canceled out of his regular Saturday night poker game, which he had never done before."

"Who was in the game?" Norah asked.

Carol answered promptly. "Old buddies from the Job. Thomas Christie, Bob Renquist, Amos Hardeen, Greg Sommers. They're the regulars. If one of them couldn't make it, it was his responsibility to provide a substitute. They took it very seriously."

"And who was your father's substitute?"

"Jack Wilmette."

Norah and Danny Neel exchanged glances. The name meant nothing to either of them, but each one made note of it anyway. Routine.

Norah closed her notebook and replaced it in her pouch. "Well, we won't trouble you any further."

"That's it?"

"Unless you have something more you want to tell us?"

"You don't want to talk to the girls?"

"What about? They were in school at the time of your father's death, weren't they?"

"Yes. Oh yes."

"Well then, they don't know anything. Why don't you bring them home? I think that would be much less stressful for them than spending the night in an unfamiliar place. I'll make sure that anyone still upstairs goes back to the squad." In the act of extending her hand, Norah changed her mind and drew the shaken woman into her arms and held her.

"Bring them home," she said.

▼ Norah and Danny had arrived in separate cars. Norah's new secondhand Volvo was the nearer, so they stopped beside it to talk. Ordinarily they would have gone back to the squad, but tonight was not ordinary.

"Why don't you come over to my place," Norah suggested. "Ferdi's there. We can talk and plan tomorrow's schedule."

The question was plain on Danny's face.

Norah answered it. "He's baby-sitting Patrick." She didn't add, "On his own time." She was not required to explain.

"I see." The young detective was definitely uncomfortable.

Norah knew why and she couldn't blame him, but it wasn't any of his business. "I'm going to need Sergeant Ciccerone's file from Personnel. Have them send it to me at the apartment tomorrow morning, ASAP. Also, would you mind picking up my fax machine and bringing it with you when you come? There'll be a lot of documents going back and forth."

"You want me to pick up the fax from your office and bring it over to your house?" Danny Neel enunciated with care. "You want me to report for duty at your apartment?"

"That's right."

"Excuse me, Lieutenant, what exactly are we after here?"

"The reason for Sergeant Ciccerone's death."

"You said yourself it can't be anything but suicide."

"Yeah, but why did he do it? There has to be a reason, Danny, and it has to be more than worry over his health. We'll give his doctor a call, but I don't think it's going to lead anywhere."

Neel frowned. He could see himself getting tied up in a procedural squabble and entangled in a case that was going nowhere. "I think the daughter believes it was suicide—in spite of all her protestations."

"She's torn. She doesn't know where her best interests are," Norah agreed.

That encouraged Neel. "I don't know what insurance Bill carried, but most policies don't pay off on suicides." He paused. "And she's had trouble with insurance companies before."

"We'll find out. That's our job." Norah raised her square chin.

The lieutenant had the bit in her teeth, Danny Neel thought with admiration. She was getting ready to run. Was it up to him to stop her? "You intend to conduct the investigation from your apartment?"

"Why not?" The chin now thrust forward.

He backed off immediately. "No reason."

"Then I'll see you in the morning."

"Yes, ma'am." He opened the car door for her, waited till she was settled behind the wheel, then shut it. But he didn't move away from the car door.

"What?"

"About the fax? Could you make out an order?"

Norah grinned. "Never mind, I'll get it myself. Lighten up, Detective. It's going to be by the book."

▼ Norah meant what she said. She had no intention of getting herself or any of her people into trouble over this. It was simply more expeditious for her to go to the office herself and pick up the machine. It was now ten-fifteen and few people would be around the squad room. In the morning she would arouse the curiosity of the entire day shift. Not that she thought she was doing something wrong. She was not stealing the machine, merely borrowing it. So, why not do it the easy way?

▼ If Fernando Arenas noticed the bundle Norah carried when she came home, he didn't identify what it was. At least, he didn't mention it. Nor did she. She set it to one side on the console in the hall and accepted Ferdi's help out of her jacket.

"How'd it go?" she asked eagerly.

"Terrific! Yankees, six to nothing. Oh, you mean with Patrick?"

"He didn't give you any trouble?"

"Slept right through. He's a great kid, Norah."

"I think so. I'll just look in on him. I'll be right back."

The room was lit only by a night-light plugged into a wall socket. It was light enough for Norah to see that Patrick was sleeping soundly. His eyes were closed and his long lashes extended over the lower lids. His blond hair was tousled. He smelled of soap and water and talcum powder. As she bent over to kiss him, he stirred. Dreaming? Then he chuckled. A good dream, Norah thought, and wished for him only good dreams. As always in such moments with her son,

Norah was filled with overwhelming gratitude. She thanked God for letting her have him and begged for help in raising him. After that she left, closing the door quietly behind her, and returned to Felix waiting in the foyer.

"Thanks, Ferdi."

"My pleasure, and I mean it. How'd it go? Open-and-shut?"

"What makes you think that?"

"When a man puts the barrel of a gun into his mouth and pulls the trigger, he's convinced me he means to destroy himself."

"When four men before him, all police officers, did the same thing, I'd say it's important to find out why."

"I thought the brass wanted to play this down," Ferdi said.

"Not anymore. They can't. Jim Felix called me early last week and asked me to visit Ellen Douglas, Sergeant Douglas's widow. That suggests there were already qualms on the fourteenth floor. It leads me to believe he'll support our investigation of the Ciccerone case. As you know, Jim's very close to the C of D."

Arenas's dark eyes were gleaming. This would be a great challenge to both of them. "How will you manage about Patrick?"

"If Mohammed won't go to the mountain, then the mountain must come to Mohammed."

"You've got that backward, haven't you?"

"We'll see."

▼ During the time Colleen Kelly lived in and cared for Patrick, Norah spent a limited amount of time with him. She saw him in the morning before she left for work. At night, she usually managed to get home just in time to be with him while he ate his supper. She put him to bed and read to him until he fell asleep. She wanted to be the last person he saw at night and the first person he saw upon waking. These two periods were the highlights of her day. Now that she was working at home and was actually with him, the bond between them should be growing stronger.

Oddly, she didn't feel as close. Her attention was distracted, Norah reasoned. There were too many interruptions. Caring for a young child while holding down a full-time job or running a business wasn't as easy as most people supposed, and now that she would be conducting a major investigation—Norah was certain the Ciccerone case would turn into just that—it could become more difficult still. She must organize her time with Patrick, not just the getting up and the going to bed, but all their time. They should take walks, play games: she would draw up a schedule.

As to the investigation, she reluctantly admitted and accepted the fact that she couldn't participate actively. She would have to be satisfied with the role of supervisor. Danny Neel would be carrying, naturally, since he had caught the squeal. For starters there should be at least two men to work with him. Who should they be?

Not Ferdi; she needed him to cover the chart and to serve as liaison. Simon Wyler? Norah had a lot of confidence in Wyler. For all the panache of his Italian suits, his wide-brimmed fedora and narrow pointed shoes, as well as his elegant manner, Simon Wyler was a sound investigator and a dogged one. He didn't accept the obvious. He didn't give up easily. Norah put his name down.

There was Julius Ochs. He had none of Wyler's flair. He was an introvert, a scholar of the justice system and a whiz at research. He was also willing to stray from the beaten path, to seek new venues. She put his name down.

▼ The next morning, Norah dressed Patrick and gave him some breakfast. She tried to eat, but her nervousness over her new work-at-home arrangement was too great. Norah put the dishes in the dishwasher and went into the living room to set up a work area. Her office away from the office, she thought.

From neighbors she borrowed a couple of folding tables and folding chairs; these would serve as desks for Wyler and Ochs. She moved a vanity table from the nanny's room to serve as Danny Neel's desk. Pushing and tugging, she rearranged the furniture to clear space for them. Sofa and end tables could stay as they were, but the coffee table and flanking armchairs had to be shoved against the wall. Her own desk, which presently faced the window and would have had her with her back to the room, she now turned around.

She had an old manual typewriter she hadn't used in years. This went to Danny. Wyler and Ochs would have to provide their own. Each man carried a cellular phone, so that was all right. She unwrapped the fax machine and placed it on her own desk. Voilà! The finishing touch.

Stepping back to admire the arrangements, Norah knew instantly what was missing—a computer. Well, how many years had they functioned without such miracles? They could do so awhile longer. By ten, she was set up and the fax was beginning to spew out paper.

CHAPTER 6

▼ Fernando Arenas was a sergeant and Lieutenant Mulcahaney was his boss. As the squad's whip, it was certainly not his place to questions her orders, but rather to implement them. He was seldom inclined to do otherwise. And he would not oppose her in this, though he thought she was making a serious mistake. It was not in Norah's nature to flout the rules, but maybe after a night's rest she would change her mind. Noting the clear space on her desk where the fax usually sat, he knew it must have been the parcel she had brought home last night. Not a good omen. But as long as the phone didn't ring, as long as she didn't call . . . there was hope.

Danny Neel burst Arenas's bubble when he reported in. "She wants Ciccerone's personnel records. She intends to keep the case open."

"It's her decision to make." Sparks flew from Arenas's eyes. He was not disposed to criticize Norah to another officer. He would certainly not allow anyone else to do it.

"So? What are you waiting for?"

The phone rang and Arenas snatched at it. "Homicide, Fourth Division. Sergeant Arenas speaking."

"It's Norah, Ferdi. Good morning. How are you?"

"Fine. How—"

"I want to tell you what I've decided," she broke in, her tone all business. From then on Arenas did nothing but listen and take notes.

Neel watched Arenas and tried to read the whip's expression. At last, Arenas hung up.

"What? What does she want?" Danny couldn't contain his curiosity.

Ferdi got up and waved to Wyler and Ochs. He waited for them.

"The lieutenant wants me with the three of you at twelve at her place." He pointed to Neel. "You're to bring Ciccerone's file along with everything else you've got on the case so far."

"She knows what I know. We interrogated the daughter together. There isn't anything else," Neel protested.

"Don't tell *me*. Tell *her*." Arenas turned to the other two. "You are to get together with whoever worked the Schiff and Douglas cases. Talk to them. If possible get copies of their DD5's and anything else you can."

"Why?" Wyler wanted to know. Norah encouraged questions. "I thought both those cases were closed. What's up?"

"You'll find out at noon. Then you'll tell me."

"That'll be the day," Ochs murmured to no one in particular.

▼ The three detectives Norah had carefully chosen arrived at her front door punctually and rang her bell. She admitted them and led them to the transformed living room. The soft gasp told her more than words could have. All at once, she saw with their eyes, realizing that the arrangements she had toiled over were inadequate, pathetically so. She refused to acknowledge it. They'd all worked under worse conditions and she was prepared to remind them of that.

"We're focusing on the Ciccerone case, but we'll also be looking into the alleged suicides of Stewart Schiff and Kevin Douglas, paying particular attention to the possibility of a link."

That got their attention, Norah thought. That diverted them from any complaints about the card tables and folding chairs.

"Danny will be carrying, so he gets the spot beside me." She pointed to the vanity table. "He also gets my second-best typewriter. The two of you can choose either table and you need to provide your own typewriter. You each own a cellular, so that's no problem. There'll be no regular shifts; we'll work as the need arises. No official overtime."

"Gee! You make it really attractive, Loo." Julius Ochs grinned, declaring his allegiance by use of the abbreviation.

Norah didn't smile back, not yet.

"Something else needs to be said. You are here to oblige me because for the moment I'm without anyone to care for Patrick. But you are not here as baby-sitters. I will never leave you alone with him. I will not burden you with responsibility for him. I will never go out for any reason unless there's a bona fide attendant with him. That's a promise. If the arrangements trouble you, say so and leave. No hard feelings." She looked directly at each man, one at a time.

"Excuse me for just a moment," she said, and left them alone.

She was giving them a chance to discuss it among themselves. Nobody had anything to say; they merely looked at each other and shrugged. They waited and soon Norah was back. She was leading a little blond boy by the hand.

He was a sturdy child, big for his age, wearing blue overalls that matched his eyes. He showed no shyness, but looked them over with great interest. A teenage girl in the uniform of the local parochial school trailed behind him.

"Gentlemen, this is Patrick. Patrick, these are my friends." Norah gave the child a gentle push forward. He responded by holding out his hand.

"Hello."

Wyler, who was nearest, beamed and took it. "Hello, Patrick." Patrick moved on to Ochs and then to Neel.

Norah introduced the girl. "This is Nancy Westphall. She's agreed to look after Patrick weekdays from twelve to six. Nancy carries a heavy study schedule and has six brothers and sisters. She is the oldest, so her mother relies on her help. She's giving us all the time she possibly can." Norah's nod indicated to the sitter she could go and take Patrick along.

Wyler waited for the door to be shut.

"It seems only yesterday you were pushing him around in a baby carriage."

"Well, it's true what they say—they grow fast."

"He's a fine boy and I wish you both every joy. We'll help in every way we can."

"Thank you, but there's something else that needs to be said. This case we're working on is not only complicated, it's extremely sensitive. We'll be interrogating colleagues and friends. We'll have to step carefully in order to avoid unfounded allegations, and at the same time press every advantage."

She paused.

"Sounds to me like a job for IA," Ochs remarked.

"IA is already in by way of the Schiff death. For the moment they're not going after the other cases. That's not to say they won't."

The men made no comment, but the looks were glum.

"The brass are concerned about these deaths," Norah went on. "They don't want them linked. 'Linked' suggests a malaise in the department which the media is already referring to as Blue Death. 'Linked' also suggests corruption, which has been wiped out, or I should say it has been declared wiped out. What the brass wants is for these deaths to be unconnected. They would really like it if it could be shown they weren't self-inflicted."

"Murder," Simon Wyler whispered.

"Far out," Neel said.

"It won't be easy," Ochs said. "Given the MO."

"When is it ever easy?" Norah commented. "I chose the three of you because I not only consider you expert investigators who will not take anything for granted, but I know you understand the present climate in the city and the department." Norah took a deep breath. "I hope I've clarified and calmed your concerns. If I haven't, we'll call it quits."

Each man there knew Norah well enough to understand that she didn't mean she would close the investigation; she'd replace him. Simon Wyler surveyed the room with the eye of a connoisseur looking at a jumble sale. He went over to the card table nearest the window and sat down on the folding chair—cautiously. It shook under him.

"This is not going to do my back any good. Do you mind if I bring in my own chair from home?"

"Bring whatever you need."

"Okay for my Tensor lamp?" Ochs asked.

"Of course."

Neel was the last to get into the spirit. "We'll need some kind of filing cabinet. There's a secondhand office supply store near my house. I'll pick up something cheap."

"Give me the bill."

"My treat, Loo." Danny now was eager to make up for his earlier, almost surly reluctance.

Norah was touched. She had expected support, yes, but this was more than she had hoped for. She swallowed. "So. We'll treat this as three separate investigations, always keeping in mind that they might become one. Let's take them in order.

"Stewart Schiff. This one's yours, Julius. Detective Tarentino doesn't appear to have dug very deep, but we know IA doesn't encourage outside investigation. They call it prying. Tarentino's young. He might have been intimidated." Julius Ochs, despite his mild, scholarly exterior, would not be, Norah was certain.

"See what you can find out."

"Right."

"Next, Kevin Douglas. Chief Felix is particularly interested in this one. He wonders if there might have been something wrong in the marriage that might have driven him to take his own life. What do you think, Simon?"

"I've heard only good," Wyler declared. "Douglas married his childhood sweetheart. They have four children. And, as we all know, he's had a phenomenal career."

"We're not looking under rocks," Norah said. "We only want to confirm what we've learned. Douglas's hobby was carpentry. He converted the basement of his house into a recreation room. Designed, drew up the plans, did the actual work himself. So he had contact with the lumber mill, hardware supply store. Did he do his own electric? How about the plumbing?"

"It must have used all his spare time," Wyler commented. "How did Mrs. Douglas feel about that? What was she doing meanwhile?"

Norah nodded. "I'll talk to the neighbors." She was silent for a few moments, settling matters in her own mind.

"Sergeant William Ciccerone. That's yours, of course, Danny. You know what the daughter said about her father. You know his reputation in the precinct. You should, however, get another point of view, probably from his poker buddies."

▼ It was in a row of tract houses in a working-class neighborhood, within sight of fields of oil storage tanks. Each house had a patch of ground front and rear, and it was in the way this small allotment of land was used that the owners were individualized. Some had gardens. They were of various kinds and pretensions. The Douglas place displayed a few well-cared-for rosebushes.

Norah parked her car a short distance from the Douglas home and then walked back to get a better look at the neighborhood. There was no activity. The sky was overcast, the air heavy. There was no incentive to sit on the stoop or play ball in the street. It didn't seem like summer. Norah gave up her tour and went directly to the Douglases' front porch and rang the doorbell. It was a considerable time before it was answered.

From what she could see through the narrow opening the door chain permitted, Ellen Douglas was very much what Norah had expected a woman carrying her fifth child and who had recently lost her husband would be. She should have been blooming, Norah thought, but her skin was sallow. Her blotchy, raw nose still dripped, and was swollen from much blowing; her eyes were red from many days of crying.

"I'm Lieutenant Mulcahaney." Norah displayed her shield case. "Chief Felix has sent me to offer condolences on behalf of Commissioner Lundy and the department."

"Oh." Ellen Douglas stood mute, the door still on the chain. After a few endless moments, she cleared her throat. "Commissioner Lundy has already been here."

That took Norah by surprise, but she covered it. "I'm here at the behest of the Chief and the Commissioner to help in any way I can."

"Thank you."

Norah waited to be asked inside. "Have I come at a bad time?"

"I was getting ready to go to the funeral parlor."

"I'd be glad to drive you there. My car is down the street."

"I've already made arrangements. A friend . . . One of my neighbors is coming to pick me up and drive me."

"I see. Well, would you prefer I come back later, after the wake?"

"People will be coming here afterwards. I don't know . . ." Ellen Douglas hesitated.

"We need to talk, Mrs. Douglas."

There was steel in Norah's voice that had not been there before, and Ellen Douglas heard it.

"If you'd like to come in now for a few minutes . . ."

"Thank you." As the chain was released and the door opened, Norah quickly stepped inside.

Ellen Douglas tried to make the best of the awkward situation. "May I offer you coffee? Tea? A cold drink? Something to eat?"

Through the open arch to the left, Norah saw a table laden with all types of foods and pastries.

"From my neighbors. Please, have something."

"Coffee then. Thank you."

Taking a cup from the sideboard, Ellen Douglas filled it from an electric percolator, before handing it to Norah. "We can go into the parlor." She led the way across the hall to what had started as a side porch and as the family grew had been closed in. It was furnished with the original wicker "set," its floral cretonne cushions badly faded. The matching drapes were too heavy for the room and shut out what light might have filtered in on a bright day. The windows were badly in need of washing. The wall-to-wall carpet showed the traffic pattern and hadn't been vacuumed for a while. Norah reminded herself of what had happened in this house recently and was ashamed to be so critical. At the same time she couldn't help but note that the dust and dirt were not the accumulation of days but an indication of chronic neglect.

The young widow appeared not to have taken much better care of herself. She had tried to make up for it with cosmetics, but had applied them with a clumsy hand. The foundation she chose was the wrong shade for her pale skin, uneven and streaked at the cheeks. Her lipstick was too dark, the eye shadow too frosty. She wore black, but the dress was too short, too tight, and had a big rhinestone clasp at the shoulder. Inappropriate, to say the least. A cocktail dress perhaps. Maybe it was all she had.

"You have four children?" Norah asked, curious about their condition.

"Yes. A boy eight, twin girls ten, and my eldest boy is fourteen. They're staying with my parents."

"And where are they?"

"Brooklyn."

Norah took no notes. In situations like this, the witness gave freer responses without the restriction of having her words recorded. Norah had a good memory and it was her practice to write up the interview as soon as she possibly could, often in her car before driving away.

"Were the children present . . . I mean, were they in the house when your husband was discovered?"

"They were upstairs in their rooms doing homework or watching TV."

"So they didn't actually see . . ."

"They saw nothing; they heard nothing."

"But they must have heard the police sirens and realized that they stopped at this house," Norah insisted gently. "Children are curious and also smart. They would have looked out the window and seen the police cars and the ambulances."

"I told them their father had an accident. He was being taken to the hospital, I said, but he would be all right. I said I was going with him and they would be staying with their grandma and grandpa—for the night anyway. They accepted it. I wish I could."

"What do you mean?"

"Kevin had been working on that stupid rumpus room or family room or whatever you want to call it for more than two years, spending every spare minute and every spare dollar on it. We never went anywhere or did anything because of it. Finally, he finishes and we throw a party to celebrate. He stocks up on the beer and peanuts and potato chips and invites his buddies. Then when everything's all set—he blows his brains out? Excuse me, Lieutenant, I don't buy it."

"May I see the room?"

Ellen Douglas frowned; then she shrugged. "This way."

They passed through the large, old-fashioned kitchen, down a steep flight of steps to the basement, and past a closed door. From behind it, Norah could hear the hum of the generator and feel the heat of the boiler. To the right was a small hallway in which two doors were set at right angles to each other. Cool air seeped in from the bottom of one. The lock of the other was splintered.

"The men broke in to get to Kevin," his widow explained. "I haven't had a chance to get it fixed."

Without comment, Norah carefully squeezed past.

The room was the size of the two front rooms upstairs combined.

It was all pickled pine paneling. The bar at one end was pickled pine. After a couple of drinks, the knotholes would make you cross-eyed. There was a sixty-cubic-inch refrigerator, state-of-the-art, and of course, the feature attraction, the giant television set. Everything was top-of-the-line. Despite the fact that he had done all the labor himself, this must have cost Kevin Douglas plenty.

Of course, photographs had been taken by the crime scene squad, and Norah had studied them closely, so she didn't need to ask the widow where they found Kevin, or in what condition. She could spare Ellen Douglas another traumatic repetition. It had all been cleaned up by now, naturally. The white chalk outline of the body, the blood and gore were gone, but Norah could visualize it right there in front of her. She could see the handsome young cop—the pride of the department, respected by the men who worked with him, admired by his neighbors—sprawled on the new sofa in front of a mammoth television screen while his life oozed out onto the fine leather.

"Was it dark?" Norah asked abruptly.

"Was what dark?"

"The television. Was it on or off?"

"I don't know. I think . . . I didn't notice, maybe it was on." She began to heave. "I'm sorry." Clasping a hand over her mouth, Ellen Douglas made a run for the newly installed bathroom.

While she waited, Norah continued to reconstruct in her mind what might have happened. According to the report submitted by Detective David Hinkley, the dead cop's partner, and the DD5's submitted by the various officers present, they had all been invited for seven o'clock to watch the hockey game on the new set. That would have been thirty-five minutes before the puck was to be dropped—plenty of time to get a buzz on. They arrived more or less promptly and waited in the upstairs parlor for the host to come and lead the way down. At seven-thirty when he hadn't shown, they decided to go and look for him.

Norah imagined Douglas sitting on this sofa, relaxing with a beer before the party. One of the crime scene shots showed a beer bottle on the cocktail table. In the same photograph, Kevin Douglas's right arm was resting along the back of the sofa, wrist limp but gun still in hand.

How did Douglas happen to have the service revolver handy? Norah asked herself. He was casually dressed in chinos and a plaid shirt. No shoulder holster. He could have had the gun tucked into his waistband, of course. But why? He was giving a party in his own home—why was he armed?

Douglas must have been waiting for someone. Not a friend, obviously.

This person had not come to the rec room through the house. Ellen had not admitted him. Kevin probably had, using the new entry which would have to open out on the backyard. Actually, it opened into the garage. There, Norah found another door and that led finally to the street. Tricky, she thought, and went back inside.

"Mrs. Douglas?" she called out.

Ellen appeared, looking drained and still not completely recovered.

"I can't seem to keep anything down."

"You should rest for a while," Norah said.

"Yes. If you'll excuse me, that's what I'll do."

They made their way back via the kitchen stairs and stopped in the entrance hall.

"Shall I see you up to your room?" Norah asked.

"No, thank you. I'm all right."

"If you think of anything else or you need anything, call me." Norah handed her one of her cards and left. She walked down to her car, got in, and drove off. She circled the block and came back from the other direction, pulled over, and waited.

After about twenty minutes, she observed a car drive into the Douglas driveway. The driver got out, walked up the steps to the house, and rang the bell. He was admitted almost immediately.

CHAPTER 7

▼ At eight the next morning, Norah's downstairs buzzer sounded. A heavy voice she didn't recognize announced he was from—a name she couldn't get and a warehouse she'd never heard of. He had a delivery for N. Mulcahaney.

"What warehouse? I'm not expecting—"

"If you're N. Mulcahaney, I've got furniture for you. You got a freight elevator in this building?"

"No, and I didn't order anything and I'm not accepting anything I didn't order."

"Fine with me. I'll leave the stuff on the sidewalk. You get the sanitation department to haul it away."

"Wait a minute. Will you please wait a minute till I come down and see what you've got?"

"Look, lady, you want the stuff or you don't want it?"

"She wants it. She wants it."

Norah recognized that voice in the background: Danny Neel.

"I want to talk to you, Danny. Danny?" But the line was dead. She could hear the whine of the elevator coming up. Norah waited at her door till it reached her floor and Danny came charging out.

"Wait till you see what I've got for us! And it's not going to cost anything. I mean it—zero, zilch, nada! They were about ready to pay us for taking it away." He grinned at Norah's expression. "Well, not quite, but it *is* free. It's got a couple of nicks and scratches here and there, but it's good, solid stuff. Trust me." He came close to patting Norah's hand. Instead, he waved to the truckers behind him. "Okay guys, down the hall. Over here. Let's go!"

Meanwhile Wyler and Ochs, having decided to walk up, arrived, sweating and out of breath. Inside her apartment, Norah's phone rang.

"Hold everything," she told Neel, and ran to pick it up in her bedroom before the recorded announcement kicked in.

"Hello?"

"Ms. Mulcahaney? This is Nancy Westphall."

"Yes, Nancy?" Norah's heart sank. The girl was scheduled to come in at twelve. This did not bode well. "Are you all right?"

"Actually, no. I have a bad cold and I'm afraid I'll pass it on to Patrick. I wouldn't want to do that."

"No, of course not. I appreciate your concern, Nancy." Norah hid her disappointment. "How long do you think your cold will last?"

"A couple of days," was the cautious reply. "I'll let you know when I feel better."

That meant she had another, better job, or she didn't feel like working. "Well, thanks for calling and get well soon."

What else could she say? Norah tried hard to keep annoyance out of her voice and to sound as pleasant and sincere as she could. Anything else would cause bad feelings and she wouldn't ever be able to hire the girl again—which she might have to do sometime. Norah slowly put the receiver back into its cradle.

As she sat on the side of the bed trying to find a way out of today's predicament, Norah heard loud voices in her living room and the bumping and thumping of furniture being moved around. For the moment, she ignored it; her top priority was to start calling around for a replacement sitter. Her list was right there beside the telephone. She pressed the keys for the first number. She was in luck; by eight-thirty she had found replacements for the next two days, but as she'd anticipated, she wasn't able to get anyone for today. That meant another day she could have Patrick all to herself.

Suddenly, she was aware of the silence in the apartment. After all the noise, it was ominous. She went out to see what was happening, and stopped short at the threshold of her living room.

The three detectives had rolled up their sleeves and literally transformed the room. Not only were the bridge tables she had borrowed gone, as well as the folding chairs and the vanity, but so was everything else. In their place was sleek, modern office equipment—desks and a file cabinet of gray metal. There was even a blackboard on its own stand.

"Where's my furniture? What have you done with it?"

Wyler and Ochs wouldn't look at her, but turned to Neel instead.

He squirmed, but finally responded. "It's in the basement. We made a deal with your super. You can leave it for as long as we're here working on the case. As soon as it's cleared, at a moment's notice you can have it back. We'll bring it up ourselves if necessary."

"You bet you will," Norah told him, steel in her voice.

"You said it was our responsibility to provide any additional equipment we might need," Danny reminded her.

"Like a couple of typewriters, or Julius's Tensor lamp, or Simon's orthopedic chair. I didn't authorize you to move me out of my home." Norah gestured helplessly as her voice broke. "The things you relegated to the basement have meaning for me."

"I'm sorry, Lieutenant. We'll bring them back up."

"What do you expect me to do with this stuff once we're through?"

Neel was momentarily stumped; he hadn't thought that far ahead. "We'll donate it to the department!"

"Suppose they don't want it?"

"Somebody will want it. I guarantee you."

Wyler stepped forward. "Look, Lieutenant, it was a dumb thing to do. We got carried away. We'll put it all back like it was." He gestured for the other two to give him a hand with the desk nearest to the door, which was to have been his.

"Wait." Norah looked around. She sighed. "As long as you've gone to all this trouble and it's set up, I suppose . . ."

"Yes!" Neel exclaimed.

"We might as well use it."

Broad grins from Wyler and Ochs.

"I'm glad you didn't get rid of my desk," Norah remarked.

"We didn't dare," Ochs said, his eyes twinkling behind the tinted lenses of his glasses.

They got down to business.

"I'll be working inside today," Norah told them. But she didn't say why, because she didn't want them to think her arrangements for Patrick were not reliable and at some time one of them might be called on to fill in.

Yesterday had been a short day, which the men had used to familiarize themselves with the assignment and to collect the reports and documents relating to what the media was now routinely referring to as the Blue Deaths. These they now turned over to Norah. Most of this morning was gone also; nevertheless, she took the time to give them a detailed account of her talk with Ellen Douglas.

"I didn't press her as to how she spent her time while her husband isolated himself in the basement. She indicated clearly she resented it."

"It appears Kevin Douglas's home life was not so perfect after all." Simon Wyler flicked a bit of fluff from the lapel of his elegant, Italian silk jacket. "It makes you wonder that they got together long enough to conceive a fifth child."

"Unless the child she's carrying isn't his," Danny Neel suggested.

Norah recalled the widow's preoccupation with her looks at a time of mourning. It didn't necessarily point to another man, but . . .

"Suppose she was having an affair and somehow Douglas found

out?" Danny warmed to his theory. "Do you think he cared enough to kill himself?"

Ochs entered the discussion. "From what I hear, his hand was quick on the trigger. I think he would have been more likely to kill one of them—his wife or her lover. Or both."

Norah let them toss it around for a while and then stepped in. "How about one of them killing him?"

▼ Across the street, the man in the gray '89 Pontiac stirred restlessly; he had been there, nearly motionless, since five P.M. He didn't like daytime work. For one thing, there were too many interruptions, too much activity, too many people moving around, coming and going. His work required quiet concentration. Furthermore, there was more terror in the night. Terror was his stock-in-trade.

The Pontiac was secondhand, unwashed, nondescript, and unlikely to be remembered. The man had selected it carefully to match his own image. He was tall and lanky and much stronger than he appeared. His skin was dusky. He might have cut an impressive figure, stood out in a crowd, but in his business that was not desirable. He had learned instead to minimize the impression he made. He avoided trendy hairstyles—ponytails, dreadlocks, shaved heads. He had his hair cut like a Wall Street businessman's and was clean-shaven. He wore metal-framed glasses with tinted lenses and a shapeless fedora with a wide brim which further served to shadow his face. His three-piece suits were knockoffs of famous designers and were a bad fit, also intentionally.

He'd had the *New York Times* spread out in front of him, but it was getting dark and anyone who chanced to notice him would wonder how he could possibly read. He folded the paper and set it aside and slumped down, prepared to spend the next hours doing nothing. He was used to it. It was part of the game, or the job—whichever, depending on how you looked at it. Patience. Patience was always rewarded.

The sun set at eight P.M. The lights came on in the fifth-floor apartment. Three hours later, they went out. He waited another fifteen minutes, then picked out her number on his cellular phone. He let it ring several times, and when she answered he hung up.

▼ At precisely 7:45 A.M. on Friday, Mrs. Ida Gantry rang the doorbell. She was fifteen minutes early. A good start, Norah thought as she let the new nanny in.

She was a portly, comfortable-looking woman in her mid-fifties with an ample bosom which she carried like a shelf in front of her. Fire engine–red hair contrasted with pasty white skin. Her voice was low and husky. She spoke with an accent Norah took to be Cockney. She had confided in the interview the day before that she and her husband, Albert, now deceased, had been in "the business." *The show business, don't you know?*

"Do you have any children, Mrs. Gantry?" Norah had asked.

"No, Lieutenant. Wanted to, but never could." Her green eyes misted. "We were on the road most of the time with a show or doing our act in the clubs. Out of one town and into another. That's no life for a child, is it? When would he go to school? How could he make friends? I prayed, but God said no. He had His reasons, I always say."

Norah was touched. "How did you come to leave England and live here?"

"My sister, Dorothy, married an American. After a few years they divorced, but she liked it here and her daughter, Alma, was very much an American, so she stayed. Right after my Bertie died, Dorothy was stricken by cancer. Alma wrote to me. Dorothy needed care. Alma would have to leave her job in order to look after her and she couldn't afford to hire anyone, so she asked me to come and help out." Deep in her memories, Mrs. Gantry paused. After a few moments, she shook herself free.

"When my Bertie was alive, we were too much on the move to make friends. We didn't need them; we had each other. With him gone, I was alone. I was glad to come. It took Dorothy thirteen months to die. In terrible pain, she was. Terrible."

"I'm so sorry," Norah murmured.

"I was with her constantly. I had a cot set up in her room and I slept at her feet. After she died, Alma asked me to stay on. I had no reason to go back, so I accepted. But now that I don't have Dorothy to look after, I have time on my hands and I don't know what to do with it. I have no job skills. Even if I could learn computers, who would hire me when there are so many smart *young* people ahead of me? I'm well fixed. I don't need the money, but I do need something to do. I do need to contribute something to somebody."

Mrs. Gantry was sent from heaven, Norah thought, and brought Patrick in to meet her. Though he no longer took an interest in the various sitters who came and then were never seen again, he examined Ida Gantry closely and allowed her to pick him up and sit him on her lap.

There was only one drawback: Mrs. Gantry couldn't work nights.

She had no job references, but she did present a letter from her pastor attesting to her good character and her work for the church.

Norah called him to confirm that he had indeed written a recommendation for an Ida Gantry, a member of his parish. She made a second call to the American Design Association to confirm that Alma Frobisher worked for them, had done so for over six years.

As she was showing the new nanny where to hang her coat, the phone rang. Norah took the call in her bedroom. It was Ferdi at the squad.

"How's it going over there? Everything okay?"

"Good. We're set up and starting to get results."

"What results?"

"It's too soon to say."

There was an awkward pause.

"Is there something specific you were calling about?" Norah asked.

"Yes. Two calls came in this morning for you. One was from Chief Felix. Call him back ASAP."

"You didn't tell him he could reach me at home?"

"I didn't know if you'd want me to."

"We're not hiding anything here, Ferdi. Particularly not from Jim Felix. What was the other call?"

"Detective Tarentino about a break-in at Irene Schiff's apartment. Ochs was asking questions . . ."

"That's right. On my orders as part of the investigation into the Blue Deaths."

"I didn't know whether you'd want me to relay the message or . . ."

"Or what? The whole point of setting this up was to facilitate communication. If you feel uncomfortable about it, I'll arrange call forwarding. Until I do, give the caller my home number."

"Yes, Lieutenant."

"We haven't got time for hurt feelings, Ferdi. Please."

"Right, Lieutenant. Same procedure for Wyler and Neel?"

"Yes, Sergeant. Where can I reach Detective Tarentino?" She jotted down the number he gave her. "I assume that's Irene Schiff's place?"

"Yes, ma'am."

"Was anything valuable taken?"

"Tarentino said not. Mrs. Schiff had been storing her former husband's papers and files till he found a larger place. The burglar went through them, but there's nothing to indicate whether he found what he wanted."

"I'll go over there myself. So if you want me, or anybody else does, that's where I'll be. After I talk to Chief Felix, of course. And Ferdi . . . I'm sorry I was testy." She hung up quickly.

It was with a slight touch of unease that Norah acknowledged to herself that she should have got back to Jim Felix long ago. She had been distracted—no, diverted—by Colleen Kelly's abrupt departure and the need to replace her. Then there was Bill Ciccerone's apparent suicide. She'd better not put it off any longer.

She gave her name to Felix's civilian secretary, who put her straight through.

"Good morning, Chief. I dropped in on Ellen Douglas the other day as you suggested. Actually, it was a couple of days ago. I should have got back to you sooner."

"Don't apologize. You have a problem, I know that. And I did say there was no urgency."

She could always count on Jim Felix, Norah thought gratefully. And all at once, the doubts she had suppressed surfaced. "Actually, there is. I have a bad feeling about the Douglas case. I'm afraid the marriage is not as ideal and serene as we originally believed."

"What makes you think that?"

"I can't put my finger on anything specific, but in view of the possibility that neither Kevin Douglas nor his widow is all we thought they were, to avoid scandal it might be wise to postpone the funeral."

Felix's shock carried over the line.

"Or we might consider scaling down the pomp and ceremony to something more private which would be less likely to be headlined by the press."

Felix sighed. "I don't know. The PC has already committed himself. If we abort or even downgrade the ceremonies, the media is going to want to know why. Frankly, Norah, we're going to need more than your 'bad feelings' as a reply."

"It will be more embarrassing if we go ahead and bury him with the bands playing, a thousand men in uniform, and an honor guard only to find out he was a crook. Or worse."

"Worse?"

"Irene Schiff's apartment has been broken into. It seems she'd been storing certain files for her ex-husband. The intruder went through them pretty thoroughly, but there's no way of knowing what he took, if anything. I'm on my way to talk to her. Would you care to come with me?"

"Do you need me?"

"I don't think so, Chief."

"Well then, you go on. By the way, how's that beautiful boy of yours? Sally keeps asking about him. As soon as she's feeling more fit, she's going to invite herself over to visit."

That was Sally Felix, Jim Felix's wife. She was recovering from a recent heart attack.

"He's healthy and happy and the joy of my life," Norah replied, and waited for some comment regarding her working out of her apartment, but Felix didn't allude to it. Was it that he didn't know or that he chose to ignore it?

CHAPTER 8

▼ The NYPD had a very active, finely tuned grapevine. Norah couldn't believe Jim Felix in his high position didn't know everything that was going on everywhere in the seventy-six precincts. By his request that she interrogate Ellen Douglas, Felix had thrown Norah the ball. She had caught it, and now Felix was giving her the opportunity to run with it. For how long? Norah wondered. That would depend on the results.

"Julius!" she called to Ochs, who was just coming in, using one of the keys she had given to each man. "What have you got on for today?"

"I was going to review the personnel files of the last three Blue Deaths." "Alleged suicides" was awkward, "victims" was harsh and didn't feel right somehow, "murders" was making too many assumptions, so they'd all adopted the media's label.

"Leave it for later," Norah said. "There's been a break-in at Irene Schiff's place. I want you to come with me."

▼ Irene Schiff lived in one of the elegant, co-op buildings that girdled Gramercy Park. Her ex had died in a modest Village walk-up. Neither Norah nor Ochs commented.

By the time they arrived and were admitted by Mrs. Schiff, the burglary squad had come and gone.

"They didn't do much," she complained.

Her pale gray eyes were magnified by granny-style glasses, the circles under them like bruises. She wore brown stretch pants, a brown-and-white-striped cotton shirt, and country boots. The room into which she ushered them was large and elegant. The furniture was Louis XV style, the accessories carefully chosen. Under the surface calm, she was agitated.

"When did you discover you'd been burglarized?" Norah asked.

"When I came in this morning," Mrs. Schiff replied. "I'd been away for a few days. We have a place up in Vermont near Manchester. We spend . . . used to spend a lot of time there, summers as well as winters. It's beautiful, secluded. Our nearest neighbor is five miles away. There's a lake. We were so happy there. I thought that maybe up there I could make contact with Stewart somehow." She turned her head away to compose herself. "I drove back this morning and walked in to all this." A sweeping gesture took in the entire room.

"It doesn't look all that bad. In fact, there doesn't appear to be anything damaged or even out of place."

"Not to you perhaps, but I could tell right away. To start with, the smell of tobacco was unmistakable. It hit me as soon as I opened the door. And look what he used for an ashtray—my lovely Bohemian glass candy dish." The small bowl she indicated held half a dozen malodorous butts. "There were other indications—a chair out of place, certain doors open that should have been shut. I'm compulsive about things being in their proper place, so my first reaction was relief that the intruder hadn't taken anything of great value. I do have some good things here. The Winslow Homer cartouche is genuine. The small Corot." she pointed. "I inherited it from my aunt in France. He might have taken those—or worse, vandalized them."

"Why do you think he would do that?" Norah asked.

"Out of frustration at not finding money or expensive electronic equipment. I've heard that happens."

"When did you call nine-one-one?" It wasn't the time Norah was after; she knew that already.

Irene Schiff understood. "As soon as I was satisfied there'd been an illegal entry. I went through the rest of the apartment and when I got to the den . . . Well, see for yourselves."

The room she showed them was so small as to be nearly claustrophobic, probably a maid's room originally. Now it served as a study and, by means of a convertible sofa, a guest room. The lack of space was cleverly turned into an asset by emphasizing it. The walls were painted a deep blue with dusky rose borders. An Oriental chest, ebony with brass hardware, stood in one corner. The lock had been smashed, one door nearly torn off its hinges. Its contents had been emptied, sheafs of papers dumped on the floor, index cards scattered.

There was no doubt that the search had centered here. Again there was the telltale stench of tobacco. The pictures on the walls were tilted crazily.

"Do you have a wall safe?"

"No."

"Is this the way you found the room?"

"More or less. The detectives from the burglary squad went through it and then the detectives from IA came."

"Did they find anything in the way of evidence? Did they take anything with them?"

"If they did, they didn't tell me," Irene Schiff said bitterly. "Frankly, Lieutenant, I was disappointed. They didn't look for evidence, or fingerprints, or anything like that. They did ask me what was missing. Since I didn't know what was here in the first place, I couldn't tell them what was missing. At that, they lost interest completely. They said they'd be in touch, but they were just going through the motions." She paused, looking first to Norah and then to Ochs for some comment, but both were silent.

"I thought since Stewart was one of theirs, they'd make an effort."

They had, Norah thought, they'd shown up. If Schiff hadn't been in IA, they wouldn't have done that much. It was the sad truth that the extent of an investigation into a burglary depended on the value of the property stolen. The new PC had indicated he was changing that and he wanted every case to be judged on its own merits. So far he hadn't indicated where the additional manpower to implement that would come from.

"Just let me review the facts, Mrs. Schiff. You and Detective Schiff have recently had an amicable divorce. He took a small apartment not so far from here and you saw each other infrequently. When he asked you to keep some papers for him, you agreed readily."

"Of course. Old case files is what he told me they were. He kept everything—every bill, every letter, whether it pertained to us, to our home, or to the Job. He was a pack rat. It's one of the things we argued about, that he refused to throw anything away. We lived in clutter." Her eyes filled. A single tear rolled down her cheek. "It doesn't seem important now."

"Would you mind if Detective Ochs stayed awhile and went through these papers and tried to make some sense out of them?"

"I'd be grateful."

"Good. One more thing before I go. Have you any idea why Stewart might have killed himself? According to the men who worked with him, he was despondent because of the divorce."

"He got over that. We both realized we had made a mistake. We were seriously thinking of getting married again."

"So he wasn't depressed?"

"Well, he might have seemed so. That was probably because he had a bad cold. Stewart took his health very seriously. He dosed himself with all kinds of nostrums."

▼ It was well after four when Norah left Irene Schiff's apartment and emerged from the building into the quiet, well-ordered square with its enclosed private park. She paused for a moment under the canopy to consider. She had left Julius Ochs behind on what was a tedious and probably hopeless quest, but the possibility that there might be a clue in that mass of paper couldn't be ignored. It would have helped to know what they were looking for, but Norah was sure Ochs had the ability to recognize it should he find it. Unless the perp had already found it. It was a real long shot, but Norah couldn't help being excited.

As she stood there uncertain what to do next, Norah glanced across the street to Gramercy Park and noticed a young woman with a child in a stroller. They were the only occupants and were about to leave. Norah continued to watch as the woman unlocked the gate, pushed the stroller through, and locked it behind them. How nice it would be, she thought, to be out like that with Patrick. But there would be other June afternoons, Norah promised herself. They had years ahead of them.

It occurred to her that she was hungry.

It was too late for lunch and too early for dinner. Instead of sitting at some counter and having a snack or a pastry she didn't want, why not go home? Patrick would be just about ready for his supper; they could eat together. Decision made, Norah stepped from the serenity of Gramercy Park into the normal pandemonium of the city. As she had come with Ochs in his car, she hailed a cab to go home. Upon arriving, she paid the driver and hurried into the building, acknowledging a neighbor's greeting as she crossed the lobby, but not stopping for any more than that. In her excitement, she had trouble putting the key in the lock of her own front door.

"Hello!" she cried out. "I'm home."

No answer.

"Hello? I'm home." Where was everybody? From where she stood, Norah could see that the living room was empty. With the new desks arranged in a row, it looked like a schoolroom without students. Where was Patrick?

"Mrs. Gantry?"

Norah hurried down the hall to the nursery. Empty. Oh God! What had happened? At that moment, she heard the front door open and close.

"Who's that?"

"It's me, Lieutenant. Ida Gantry." The woman's blowsy face was flushed by the sun. She held Patrick by the hand. "Is something wrong?"

At the sight of the boy, sturdy in his denim overalls, jacket, and railway engineer's cap, Norah's heart turned over. She knelt on one knee, hugged him, and held him close.

"I'm sorry you were upset, Lieutenant. It's such a beautiful day, I thought we should take a walk in the park," Mrs. Gantry explained. "We saw squirrels and pigeons, and had a ride on the carousel."

Norah sighed. "I didn't know what to think. Next time leave me a note, please."

"You can be sure of it, Lieutenant." Ida Gantry was contrite. Then her face cleared. "I'll be making his supper soon. Can I fix something for you?"

"Don't trouble. I'll just have a cup of coffee for now."

"There's some nice ham in the fridge. How about a grilled ham and cheese? Or an omelet?"

"Well . . ."

"Sooner done than said." Ida Gantry chuckled, her green eyes sparkling. "Why don't you get Patrick into his jammies? By then I'll have everything ready."

When Norah had tended to Patrick, she led him to the kitchen to find Danny Neel comfortably settled.

"I invited Detective Neel to have a sandwich with us. I told him you wouldn't mind," Ida Gantry proclaimed blithely.

"Of course not." The kitchen was spacious with big old-fashioned cupboards all around and a modern butcher-block table in the center. "Sit over here, Danny." Norah indicated the place. "With Patrick."

It wasn't long before Wyler arrived and joined them.

Because of Mrs. Gantry's presence and Patrick's, the case was not discussed, but even when they left, the restraint persisted.

"I could get used to this," Wyler proclaimed. He patted his mouth with a napkin and sighed his satisfaction. "But . . . back to the salt mines." He stood up.

"Stay for a moment, Simon. You too, Danny," Norah urged. "Julie and I talked to Irene Schiff this morning. According to her, Stewart was in good spirits before his death. He had a cold, but it was nothing serious. As for his being dejected over the divorce, that's way off. The truth is that she and Stewart were getting together and seriously thinking of remarrying."

"Interesting," Wyler commented.

"It sure was a well-kept secret," Neel remarked.

"I don't know that it was a secret," Norah said. "Schiff was a very private person. He wasn't in the habit of talking about himself."

"So we have to find another motive for his suicide," Neel muttered.

"*Alleged* suicide," Wyler corrected.

"Okay, alleged." Neel took the correction with bad grace. "Did Mrs. Schiff offer any other insights?"

"She answered questions," Norah replied. "Are you implying she wasn't telling the truth? Why should she lie?"

Neel shrugged.

He was obviously peeved and Norah thought she understood why. Danny had expected to be in charge of the entire case—all parts of it: under her direction, but the second chair. He was disappointed that she had called in others, though they were buddies.

"It's too early to speculate," she said, putting an end to the discussion. "I just want to let you know that another avenue for investigation has been opened. We mustn't restrict ourselves to reviewing what others have done. We've got to start fresh. Get our own perspective."

They'd be on this one forever, Danny Neel thought. "I've got a date with Bill Ciccerone's doctor tomorrow."

"I'm meeting with Dave Hinkley, Douglas's partner, later tonight," Wyler said. "They were together over four years. If there's anything going on that isn't kosher, he's the one most likely to know about it."

"Good. Good. I expect to be in the rest of the evening, so call if you need me. Oh, and one more thing. I've suggested to Chief Felix that the Douglas funeral be postponed."

Their reaction was one of stunned silence.

"How about Ciccerone? Did you ask for a delay of his funeral also?" Danny asked with some of his usual assertiveness.

"Not yet, but I will if it becomes necessary."

"Right." Neel broke into a big grin. The lieut was smart, and she wasn't afraid of anyone.

CHAPTER 9

▼ Patrick had long since been tucked in for the night. Mrs. Gantry was gone and so were the men. Norah checked the doors, front and back, made sure the windows were shut, and put out the lights—except for the bedroom light and the desk lamp. It was a set routine which calmed her and gave her a sense of security. She found the quiet of the night soothing. It was then her thoughts were clearest. So, as she had done many times before, Norah sat at her desk and let her mind wander.

She had now had the opportunity to interrogate a major figure in each of the most recent Blue Deaths, and the men had turned in their preliminary reports. It was time to evaluate their findings and compare them to hers.

Julius Ochs had done a fine job on the Schiff papers, organizing them by subject and date and cross-indexing the principal participants. This procedure often resulted in startling revelations, but not this time. Norah felt the customary tension at the base of her neck and leaned back to ease it. She had only been working a couple of hours. The night was young.

Simon Wyler called in at ten-thirty to report on his interview with Dave Hinkley. Hinkley had hinted that there was talk around the neighborhood where the Douglases lived that not everything was idyllic between them.

"There's definitely another woman involved, but Hinkley won't say more. They're closing ranks."

"Maybe I should see what I can do? Woman to woman," Norah suggested.

▼ After a spell of fine weather, it had turned cold and rainy again. Nevertheless Mrs. Gantry arrived early as before and Norah was ready for her, dressed and waiting. She was wearing black pants and pullover and over them a bright yellow slicker. She carried an umbrella but knew it would be useless when the first gust of the nor'easter turned it inside out. What a summer! she thought as another gust nearly wrenched the car door out of her hands.

By the time she reached Howard Beach, the ferocity of the storm had abated, temporarily at least. She parked as before a block away, though there was plenty of space closer by. The area had been depressing enough in fine weather; now it was utterly forlorn. Never mind, Norah thought; the good thing about bad weather was that it kept a lot of people home—particularly housewives, she hoped. And as it turned out, they were home but reluctant to admit her. When they did let her in, they were unresponsive. After two, very brief, unproductive interviews, the word must have gone out, because at the third house no one answered the bell, nor at the fourth. At the fifth she saw the edge of a lace curtain at the front window move. She rang again, insistently, then went over and tapped the window. Having caught the attention of the occupant, Norah held up her ID case. The woman nodded and came around finally to open the door.

"What can I do for you, Officer?"

According to Norah's list, this was Mrs. Edna Haig. She was in her mid-thirties. Her face was too long, her nose slightly hooked. When she smiled her teeth, startling in their whiteness, jutted too prominently. Yet there was an arresting intensity about her, a hint of banked fires that once perceived might prove irresistible to a man, Norah thought.

Mrs. Haig had let Norah in out of the rain but was not inclined to allow her past the vestibule, not even after she had identified herself and explained what she was after. It was at that point, in fact, that she became distinctly antagonistic. She assured Norah that she knew nothing about what had happened across the street. She had neither seen nor heard anything that might be relevant.

"We don't socialize with the Douglases, Herbert and me," she insisted. "So I can't tell you what goes on at those parties."

For "We don't socialize," read *We aren't invited*. Norah pounced. "What kind of parties?"

"Loud parties. Brawls. Music blaring till one and two in the morning. Summer and winter and every holiday. Cops shouldn't behave like that." She pursed her lips.

Norah let that go, temporarily anyway. "What about the children? You do have children, don't you?" Based on his interview the night before with Dave Hinkley, Wyler had provided her with a few facts and some background on the Douglases' neighbors. "They do go to the same school as the Douglas children?"

"There are over six hundred children in that school. I am not acquainted with all of their parents."

"You live across the street from Ellen Douglas."

"That makes us neighbors, not necessarily friends."

True enough, Norah thought. "You can't help but notice their comings and goings."

"I can if I'm not at home."

"That would be asking too much," Norah agreed. "Well, thank you for your time. If you should happen to think of anything later on that might be helpful, here's my card. Don't hesitate to call at any hour."

Edna Haig took it without looking at it; she was studying Norah.

"You might want to talk to a close friend of Mrs. Douglas's. She lives down the block. The corner house."

It wasn't clear to Norah what Mrs. Haig's motive was in giving this information to her. It was not likely benevolent. Attempts to harm were more revealing than those to do good, so Norah had high expectations as she bowed her head into the rain and headed for the house Edna Haig had pointed out to her. She climbed to the porch, a carbon copy of all the other porches, and rang the bell. Standing there in her yellow slicker, the only person outside, Norah felt the eyes of the woman watching her. Sighing, she thought of a better way. She returned to her car and consulted Wyler's list. There it was—Paul and Melody Lutz. She got her cellular phone out of the glove compartment and made the call.

The phone was answered right away.

"Mrs. Lutz? I'm Lieutenant Mulcahaney from the Fourth Division," Norah began in her most low-key and reassuring manner. "I understand you're good friends with Mrs. Douglas."

"Who tells you that?"

The voice was light, musical. There was a slight foreign accent which Norah couldn't place. The retort was unexpected.

"A neighbor," Norah replied as she got out of the car and started back to the corner house. "You're both married to police officers; you live practically next door to each other; it follows that you should be friends. Do you deny it?"

"Of course not."

"Well then, do you want to help your friend?"

"How can I help her? She's lost her husband. What can anyone do for her?"

It would be a big advantage to get Mrs. Lutz into a dialogue, Norah thought. "We need to talk, Mrs. Lutz. We can't this way. Please let me in." Norah's head and feet were soaked. Water had found its way inside the collar of her slicker and was trickling down her spine. The dial tone buzzed in her ears. That only made her more determined. She tried the number again, but this time there was no answer. Norah let it ring and go on ringing. She counted to twenty. Which one would break first?

At the twenty-first ring, the front door opened slowly.

"Come in."

She was much younger than Norah had thought from the brief glimpse she'd had of her through the window, and pretty too, with the stressed, burnt-out look the young affected these days. She was very thin. Her face was dead white. Her dark eyes—her dominant feature—were smudged with gray and outlined with kohl. Her full lips were covered with purple lipstick, and her long black hair hung straight well below her shoulders. The dress she wore was long, black, and unadorned, and relied on her young body to give it shape.

"I'm afraid I'm dripping all over your floor," Norah apologized. "Can we dispose of this?" She held out the wreck of her umbrella. As she did so, she got a closer look at the young woman. Yes, the dark shadow under her makeup was a bruise.

Norah took off the slicker. "If I could just shake this out somewhere? The kitchen? Or the bathroom?"

"The back porch. Give it to me."

"Sorry to be so much trouble."

Without making the polite denial which would not have been true, Melody Lutz took the coat and the ruined umbrella from Norah and carried them through the dining room and a swinging door into what had to be the kitchen. Norah looked around. The entry in which she stood was papered in a large floral print, red and yellow being the dominant colors. The same paper was on the staircase wall. Overwhelming.

She strolled into the parlor opposite. The furniture looked like it had come from the Old Country. A television set was the only indication of the twentieth century. It still used rabbit ears to bring in the picture.

"No more tricks, Lieutenant." Melody Lutz was back. "What do you want?"

"Tricks?"

"As you pointed out, I'm married to a police officer, so I know how you do things. Whatever you're after, you'll have to ask my husband."

Norah was taken aback. "Do you really want me to go to him? You say you're close friends with Ellen Douglas, but rumors are flying all over the neighborhood that you and Kevin Douglas were having an affair." She was exaggerating. Would the witness bite?

"Do you listen to rumors, Lieutenant?"

"Rumors aren't necessarily false," Norah pointed out. "Often they are signposts to the truth. Rumors are started by envious people. In this case it might be a housewife jealous of Ellen and Kevin Douglas's happiness." She thought of Edna Haig. "Usually, they are not made out of whole cloth. There's at least a grain of sand to irritate the oyster."

"There are plenty of jealous people around here, you're right about that." Melody was bitter.

"They hint that remodeling the basement was a cover for your meetings." Norah would have said it was not possible for Melody Lutz to turn any whiter, but she did.

"That's crazy! Suppose Ellen had taken it into her head to come down? It would have been much too risky. You can't prove it."

"So it's true."

"No, I didn't say that. I said—"

"Rumor also has it that your husband found out about the affair, gave you a thorough beating, and threatened to kill the two of you if it didn't stop." Norah continued to reason from what Edna Haig had hinted and the well-covered bruise on Melody's face. Melody's denials were actually helping.

Realizing that she was digging herself deeper and deeper, the young wife clamped her jaw shut and sat down. She gulped and began over again.

"Paul, my husband, is very jealous. I can't look at another man without his imagining there's something going on between us. In fact, I had to quit my job because of his jealousy. I had a good job as a model for a fashion house on Seventh Avenue. Paul got it into his head that I was playing around with one of the bosses. We were working late one night and when we came down in the elevator together, Paul was lurking in the lobby. He jumped Mr. Levinson and beat him senseless."

"Did your boss bring charges?"

"No."

"Why not?"

"Because Paul threatened to kill him. That was one thing. The other was—I wouldn't have dared support the charges. He would have killed me too. Of course, I couldn't work there anymore."

"How long had you been married when this occurred?"

"Three months."

The honeymoon hadn't lasted long, Norah thought. "What happened after you left your job?"

"He moved us out here to this godforsaken spot."

"And you met Ellen Douglas and became friends. Did you go out together as couples?"

"Occasionally. We had dinner out, went to the movies, bowling. Sure."

"When the men's time off coincided, naturally."

"Naturally."

"Was that often?"

"Depends what you call often."

"No more hedging, Mrs. Lutz, please."

"We'd get together every couple of weeks."

"When did the friendship start to sour?"

"When I got pregnant."

"Why?"

"You should be able to figure that out, Lieutenant." She shrugged. "I guess you need to hear it from me. All right. When he found out we were to have a child, Paul was ecstatic. He was good to me, couldn't do enough for me. But that didn't last. He began to brood. He accused me of cheating on him and of bearing another man's child. He slapped me around, but he didn't hurt me. Finally he put a name to the man he suspected—Kevin Douglas. Then he beat me good. He wanted me to admit Kevin was the father. I did. To stop the beating. I lost the baby, of course."

"I'm sorry," Norah said.

"I lost my baby and I lost my friend. Paul told Ellen that Kevin and I were having an affair and Ellen believed it. Naturally, she didn't want to have anything more to do with me."

▼ The rain had stopped, but it was only temporary; the sky remained ominously dark and angry. When was it they had last seen the sun? Days ago. In fact, the weather seemed to be a doleful accompaniment to this distressing case. To get to her car, Norah had to pick her way around and over puddles and jump across overflowing gutters. In no time her boots, which were supposed to be waterproof, were soaking, and she was sweating under the yellow slicker. Nevertheless, it was a relief to get out of the Lutz house.

How perversely we create anguish for ourselves, Norah thought, as the various parts of this particular puzzle fell into place. Paul Lutz, born in Poland and brought to America as an infant, dreamed of going back someday to find his roots. By living at home with his mother, by restricting himself in all but the most necessary expenses, he had saved enough so that he could have gone long since, but going was no longer enough. He'd wanted to arrive like a prince, to be what his people over there expected.

In Krakow, he met Erminia, now called Melody, and fell in love. He was old for her, but not too old by European standards. She had lived almost her entire life under the shadow of Communist oppression and Paul Lutz offered her a chance to get away. Tacitly, they made a deal. They married and Paul wasted no time bringing her back to New York and showing her off.

She made a hit right away. Everybody liked her. She changed her name to Melody and got the job modeling for the fashion house. They should have been happy, and they were until Paul became so uncontrollably jealous. He started to criticize her, belittle her looks and her enthusiasms. He wouldn't acknowledge her success but instead accused her of dispensing sexual favors in order to get ahead.

Just as Norah reached her car, a bolt of lightning split the sky and was almost immediately followed by a shattering clap of thunder. She put the key in the lock of the car door, but the rain came down before she could get it open. Hail hit the hood of the car like a spate of bullets and peppered her as she struggled against the wind to get inside. The street became a river. Her inclination was to sit it out. Her mind returned to the recent interview of Melody Lutz.

Norah didn't know what to believe. There were many possible interpretations of the young woman's story. The only person who could confirm or deny it, Kevin Douglas, was dead. If you accepted that there had been an affair, then you had choices—Paul Lutz killed Kevin Douglas for revenge; Melody killed him because they were breaking up; Ellen Douglas killed him because he had cheated on her. However you looked at it, the case for murder rather than suicide was strengthened.

The case was opening faster than she had dared hope. They now had strong indications that neither Stewart Schiff nor Kevin Douglas were suicides. That was what Jim Felix had hinted both the PC and the mayor wanted. Having got this far, Norah knew they would want more—a solution for the Ciccerone case. She herself would not be satisfied with less.

Suddenly, she was aware that the waters around her had risen alarmingly. She put the key in the ignition and turned it; the motor engaged; she edged out into the middle of the road and slowly, cautiously, headed for home.

▼ They were in the apartment ahead of her—Neel, Wyler, and Ochs—waiting. With them was Ida Gantry.

"We were worried, Lieutenant," she said.

"I'm sorry," Norah apologized to all. "The roads . . . Well, you've been out there." She turned to address the nanny. "Mrs. Gantry, would you mind waiting just five minutes more till I get into something dry?"

"Captain Jacoby has been calling, Lieutenant," Wyler informed her. "Several times. You're to get back to him ASAP."

"Oh? Did he say what it was about?"

"Only that it's urgent."

"Well, in that case, I'd better not waste any time." She headed for the telephone on her desk.

"You want us to wait, Loo?" Danny Neel asked.

Norah looked at her watch: seven o'clock. "Is there anything that can't hold over till the morning? . . . No?"

"Patrick's had his dinner and is in bed." Mrs. Gantry was eager to be on her way.

The phone rang and she snatched it up. "Oh, good evening, Captain." With her free hand she waved goodnight to all of them.

"How's it going, Lieutenant?" Jacoby asked.

"Good, Captain. Very good. We're making progress."

"I'm glad to hear it."

Captain Emanuel Jacoby did not sound glad. She waited.

"How's the situation at home?"

"I've got an excellent woman for weekdays, but I need somebody for nights and weekends. I need somebody full-time, to live in."

"I need somebody full-time over here too," Jacoby said.

Norah flushed. She'd walked right into that one. "I'm doing my best, Captain."

"I hear disturbing rumors, Lieutenant."

"What kind of rumors?"

"That you've moved the squad into your home."

"No. Oh no, Captain. What I've done . . . It was when we took on the Ciccerone case. I thought it would facilitate communications if Detective Neel, who is carrying, could report to me directly."

"I haven't seen either Wyler or Ochs around for about a week. Sergeant Arenas tells me they're over there with you. Are they on leave?"

"No, sir, they're not on leave." She knew Ferdi had stalled as long as he could. "And yes, sir, they are working on the case with me."

"Did you get authorization for any of this?"

Norah hesitated. This was her chance to bring Jim Felix into it and shift the responsibility. "No, sir."

"Don't you think you should have informed me of your intentions? At the very least you should have done that."

"Yes, sir, I should." They both knew she hadn't because he would have opposed the idea and made it impossible to implement.

"I thought we trusted each other, Norah." Jacoby was plaintive.

"I'm sorry, Captain." She had an inspiration. "Why don't you come over and see the setup? I'm sure you'll approve."

"All right. I'm on my way."

Norah was stunned. Accustomed to Jacoby's inertia, she hadn't expected him to take her up on her offer. So now she scurried around straightening up a few things, but not too many. The room should look like a workplace, not a stage set. When she was done, she went to the nursery to check on Patrick. For a moment she lost herself in the joy of having him there; then she went back to the living room turned squad room to wait. She hadn't been this nervous since taking the oral part of the lieutenant's exam. The sound of the downstairs buzzer jerked her to her feet.

It was the captain, and she buzzed him in and went to the corridor to greet him when he came out of the elevator.

"This way, Captain."

He entered the apartment ahead of her. At the living room he stopped so abruptly that she almost ran into him.

"I can't believe this."

The tone did not indicate approval and certainly not admiration.

Norah stepped around so she could see Jacoby's face.

"What do you think you're doing here, Lieutenant? Going into business for yourself?"

She was shocked. "No, Captain. Of course not."

"That's what it looks like."

"This furniture—Detective Neel got it for free. It was overstock. There was no room in the warehouse and they were going to throw it out. Honestly, Captain."

"Even if I could believe you . . ."

"Have I ever lied to you, Captain?" Norah was hurt and on the verge of getting angry. "Why would I lie?"

"Maybe you're getting a payoff."

"From whom? For what? For God's sake, Captain! You've known me long enough . . . I thought you knew me well enough . . ." She sputtered, then threw up her hands. "If I were doing something wrong, would I invite you over here?"

Jacoby didn't answer right away. Walking slowly, weight forward on the balls of his small feet, picking his way as though through a minefield, the commander of the Two-Oh examined each desk, the filing cabinet, the two battered typewriters. He stopped at the desk that was obviously Norah's. He pointed at the fax and the three telephones, one a land line and the other two cellulars.

"Neel didn't provide those."

"No, sir. The land line is an extension of my home telephone. One of the cellulars is mine, and the other, along with the fax, I brought from the office. I was the only one using them there and I will be the only one using them here."

"That may be, but they are not your property and you'll have to return them. ASAP, Lieutenant."

"Yes, sir," she agreed quickly. It looked like she was going to get off easily.

She was wrong.

"How's the case coming?"

"Good. It looks good." Some of her earlier optimism and excitement returned. "We think we can rule out depression over his divorce as the cause of Detective Schiff's presumed suicide."

"Why?"

"He and his ex intended to remarry."

"Interesting."

"There's an emotional tangle at the core of the Douglas death that suggests he was murdered either by his lover, her husband, or his wife. As for Sergeant Ciccerone, he had a chronic heart condition. According to his doctor, it was under control. That doesn't mean he didn't take it seriously. We'll talk to his buddies to find out just how seriously." She paused, expecting some comment, but there was none.

"Meantime, I've asked for the Douglas and now the Ciccerone funeral to be postponed just in case we need another look at the bodies, and to avoid embarrassment if it turns out there's some kind of corruption festering that ties them together. I'll need more people, of course."

Jacoby almost smiled. Mulcahaney had converted weakness into strength. He was not surprised. Nevertheless . . . "Out of the question, Lieutenant. You can stay on the case, but be prepared to cover the chart as usual and work out of the precinct as usual."

Norah swallowed. "I can't do that, Captain. I can't. I can't leave my baby in just any stranger's care."

"Police investigation is not a cottage industry, Lieutenant Mulcahaney. I put it to you once again: Did you get any kind of authorization from anybody to set up like this?"

Norah squared her shoulders and thrust out her chin. "I didn't think I needed it."

"Come on, Lieutenant, you've been around too long to expect me to buy that."

She sighed. "I guess I got carried away."

"I guess you did." This was what came of hiring women, Jacoby thought, but kept it to himself. "Either report for work tomorrow at the precinct, or expect to be suspended."

Norah gasped.

"That would look very bad on your record, of course. You couldn't expect much advancement afterwards, if any."

She bowed her head.

"You could duck the whole thing by taking a leave. On the other hand, this is not a good time for you to be away. They'll be making the appointments for new captains any day and you're right at the top of the list."

Norah didn't ask how he knew. She didn't doubt his sources.

Jacoby sensed he had reached her. "In fact, I was hoping . . . As you know, my health isn't good. I can't handle the work single-handedly anymore. I was hoping we could share the job. I've made an official request."

"I'm honored, Captain. I appreciate your confidence. Thank you, but I can't abandon my son."

"Damn it, Norah. Don't be so dramatic!" Captain Jacoby flared up in a rare display of temper. "I suggested day care as a possible, short-term solution to your problem. Have you even looked into it?"

"No. I'm sorry, Captain, but there's no point; I'm not giving him up." Her strong chin remained set, but tears quivered in her eyes. "I'm not putting him through what poor little Mark went through. Patrick is staying in his own home till I can find the right nanny, and I'm staying with him for as long as it takes. Even if it means resigning."

"Take it easy, Norah. Nobody's talking about resigning either. I'm just telling you what the situation is. Okay?"

"Are you taking me off the case, Captain?" she asked bluntly.

"That's not my decision," he retorted. "I am, however, ordering Ochs, Wyler, and Neel back to their regular shifts at the precinct."

He might as well have taken her off, Norah thought.

CHAPTER 10

▼ It was Sunday. Mrs. Gantry didn't come weekends. By now the men—Neel, Wyler, and Ochs—had received their orders and had been reporting to the precinct, so they wouldn't be coming. That meant she could spend the whole day with Patrick. If the weather was good—and they were certainly due for some good weather—she would take him to the zoo. If not they would try the Museum of Natural History and the dinosaur exhibit. What would Patrick make of them? Norah wondered. She had fallen asleep with visions of him standing in awe but unafraid and looking up at the prehistoric animals.

She had slept to the accompaniment of light rain on the air conditioner casing, but wakened to the harsh rasp of the downstairs buzzer.

Norah jumped out of bed, reached for her robe, and ran barefooted to the house phone in the kitchen.

"Yes?" she gasped.

"Mulcahaney? This is Tri-State Movers. You got furniture going?"

"Furniture?" Her mind was blank.

"Right. Three desks, one filing cabinet, three chairs."

"Oh, those. Yes. But this is Sunday."

"That's right, lady, and we're on overtime, so you gonna let us in or what?"

For answer, she pressed the button that would release the lock on the entrance door downstairs. So soon, she thought; she hadn't expected Jacoby to move so fast. She had just hung up when the buzzer sounded again.

"Yes?"

"Sorry to disturb you, Lieutenant. It's Danny. Is it okay for us to come up?"

Norah glanced at the kitchen clock: seven-thirty. She had hoped to sleep a little later, but Patrick would be wanting her soon anyway. "Sure, come on." The more the merrier, she thought.

The next thing she knew, two men in gray jumpsuits with *Tri-City Movers* in red letters across their backs pushed past her into the apartment. One was big and burly. The other trailing behind was as stunted as Quasimodo and had a face like a gnarled oak. He pushed a heavy dolly in front of him.

"Everything goes?" Number One asked, as he tilted Norah's desk at one end while Number Two slipped the dolly underneath.

"No no!" she cried out. "That stays."

"Why didn't you say so? Okay, lady, so you point out what you want us to take."

Danny Neel strode in. "Keep your shirt on, buddy. I'll show you."

Wyler followed Neel in.

"Sorry to disturb you on your Sunday, Lieutenant, but they're booked for all of next week," Wyler explained.

"Morning, Lieutenant. We came to give you a hand." Ochs completed the trio.

They were dressed for the job. Simon Wyler wore his version of casual: black pipestem trousers and a beige cotton work shirt topped by a Norwegian fisherman's sweater. Neel was prepared in chinos and a zippered, reversible jacket. Julius Ochs wore old clothes— things that should have been discarded long ago. Paint spatters on the baggy pants indicated he had a more realistic idea of what the job entailed than the other two.

"Thank you," Norah said. "I appreciate it, but it's not necessary. I can manage."

"Yes, Loo, it is necessary," Wyler asserted gravely and for the three of them.

Norah always had a good rapport with her people, but she was touched by this very special showing of friendship. She stood to one side and watched while the detectives along with the movers went to work. She hadn't wanted her home turned upside down; she hadn't wanted this stuff moved in. Now she was sad to see it going. She went into the bedroom for her purse, intending to tip the movers, but when she came back everyone was gone. Forlorn, she surveyed the nearly empty room. How had she ever got herself into this mess? Being Norah, the next question followed inevitably: How was she going to get herself out of it?

"Lieutenant? You want to tell us where this stuff goes?"

The detectives were bringing her things up from the basement. There was Joe's old leather club chair; the big, round copper-topped coffee table, a wedding gift from her father; lamps; two more easy chairs. "You didn't have to . . ."

"I promised you we'd put everything back like it was," Danny reminded her.

"Thanks."

"What about all this?" He indicated the pile of files and reports, the contents of the filing cabinet that had accumulated in the short time they'd been operating. "What should we do with it?"

"Take it with you; it's part of the investigation. And take the fax and the cellular. I won't be needing either for a while."

"I'm sorry, Loo." Neel bowed his head.

"For what? You got some office equipment we sorely needed. That's all. By the way, what's going to happen to it?"

"It's going to the St. James School on Fourteenth. They can use it."

"Good." Norah nodded and surveyed the room.

"Is it the way it was?" Wyler asked softly.

She wanted to say, *No, it never can be,* but she couldn't hurt them like that. She nodded instead. "Thanks."

It was time to go. They lined up at the door. Wyler held out his hand.

"If there's anything you need . . ."

Ochs was next. "If there's anything you want done . . ."

"I'll ask," she finished for them. But, of course, she wouldn't. She wouldn't put them in a position that would be a test of loyalty to her at the risk of their jobs.

The embarrassment grew.

"Hope it all gets straightened out real soon, Loo."

"Be seeing you."

They filed out with Danny Neel last. "I almost forgot—this is for you. I compiled it on your instructions while you were heading the Ciccerone investigation." He slipped her a small piece of paper folded over and over into a palm-sized square. "There's the elevator," he said, and ran.

Norah waited till the doors closed and she heard the whine of the car's descent before closing the door of the apartment. She walked back to her desk in its old position and sat down. She was alone. She felt strange, unsure of her status, but that would pass. She unfolded the paper Danny had pressed into her hand. Four names were written on it, each accompanied by an address and telephone number.

THOMAS CHRISTIE

BOB RENQUIST

AMOS HARDEEN

GREG SOMMERS

Saturday nights by turn.

Danny Neel was ambitious and he had a shrewd sense of what would be to his advantage and what would be detrimental. His passing Norah that information was almost taking sides. Wyler and Ochs had also made a commitment, though Norah would never hold them to it.

With the dismantling of the home office and the replacement of her furniture, it seemed to Norah the case had fragmented back into its separate parts. She assumed each part would continue to be carried by the detective who had originally caught the squeal, in tandem with a man from the precinct, and the assignments would remain as she had made them. There would have to be some form of central control, and she had hoped to provide it. She believed she still could. To make sure, she would call Jim Felix in the morning. First thing.

Meantime, Patrick must be getting hungry.

▼ "He's got a full schedule this morning, Lieutenant," Paula Lawson, Chief Felix's head of staff, told Norah. "He hasn't been feeling so well, so I'm trying to get him to go home after lunch." Though Lawson had been with Chief Felix only a short time, she was aware of the strong tie between her boss and Lieutenant Mulcahaney. She was envious but she hid it. "If you want to take a chance and come over and wait, I'll try to fit you in."

"I'll do that. Thanks, Paula."

When Norah arrived at One Police Plaza, she picked up a pass at the reception desk and proceeded to the fourteenth floor. She found Chief Felix's office waiting room nearly empty. It filled and emptied again, but she wasn't called. Having mentally rehearsed what she intended to say, Norah closed her eyes and relaxed completely.

"Lieutenant? Lieutenant Mulcahaney?" Norah's head jerked up. "The Chief will see you now."

"Thank you." Aware of Lawson's disapproval and the snickers of the men still waiting their turn, Norah shook her head to clear it, got up, and walked steadily into Felix's office.

He didn't look at all well. She noted it right away, and would have even if Paula Lawson hadn't mentioned it. To start with, his color was bad. Normally ruddy, he looked a sickly yellow. His green eyes, usually so sharp and penetrating, and missing nothing, were clouded and bloodshot. The corona of white hair was dingy. He had lost weight. His left hand shook.

"What's this I hear about you, Norah?"

Not an auspicious beginning, she thought. "I don't know, sir. Regarding what?"

"Don't play games with me, Lieutenant," Felix snapped.

"I didn't mean to, Chief. I'm sorry if it looks that way."

He was instantly contrite. "I know you didn't. I've got a lot on my mind these days." He waved her to a chair.

He was certainly nervous, Norah thought. He kept looking over one shoulder and then the other as though he expected someone to be there.

"Excuse me, Chief, but are you all right?"

"I'm fine." Suddenly he looked straight at her and smiled in the old way. "Let's see if we can't solve your little problem."

Norah returned the smile and relaxed. She plunged into an account of the Ciccerone case, pointing out that it came within the jurisdiction of her squad and that one of her people had routinely responded to the original complaint. As diplomatically as possible, she reminded the Chief that her visit to Mrs. Douglas and the subsequent revelations were the result of his specific suggestion. She thought that would be the clincher, but he waved it aside.

"I didn't authorize a splinter group. I'm sorry, Norah. If you'd come to me first and in view of your personal situation requested permission to work out of your home, I could have appointed a special task force and put you at the head of it. If I do that now, it will look as though you're being rewarded for insubordination."

"It was never that!" she exclaimed.

"You and I know it wasn't, but that's how it's going to look, and just now the PC is very concerned about appearances." He looked off into space for a few moments. "Your suggestion that the Douglas funeral be postponed didn't go down well with the PC either. A firm date has now been set for a week from this Thursday. The PC wanted to go with the original date. I wanted to keep it open-ended. This was a compromise."

His telling her this was an indication that Felix was on her side. It was also a warning that time was running out. He was urging her to act while at the same time putting obstacles in her path. That was politics, and Norah had learned to accept it.

"What's going to happen now?" Norah asked.

But Felix was looking off over his shoulder again. His long, narrow face glistened with sweat.

"Chief? Jim?"

Trying to clear his throat, he coughed instead. He coughed again, a spasm of coughing. His face turned a deep, mottled red. He was choking. Alarmed, Norah got up. She had to do something. What? The Heimlich maneuver? As she approached Felix and prepared to execute it, he stopped retching and gradually calmed.

"Are you all right?" Norah asked a second time. "You gave me such a scare."

"I choked on my saliva of all things. Don't look so worried. It happens."

"Are you sure?"

"Of course." There was a touch of impatience in the assurance. "It's the damn medication." Opening the center drawer of his desk, Jim Felix took out a plastic container, twisted the top off, and shook a couple of capsules into the palm of his hand. From the carafe at the corner of his desk, he poured a glass of water, put the pills in his mouth, and washed them down.

"Antibiotics," he told Norah, and read from the label, 'May result in dizziness, drowsiness, or disorientation.' I'm experiencing all of the above. I'm supposed to take a series of two three times a day for ten days. I can't wait to be through with them."

"You should go home, Jim."

"Yes, yes. I intend to. You're right. As soon as we firm up this task force and choose someone to head it. I have no idea who the PC will want." He reached out across the desk. "Come back to us soon, Norah."

She took his hand. It was cold and clammy.

▼ The interview had shaken Norah. It was the first time Jim Felix had failed to come to her aid, but that was not what troubled her most. He was not himself. He probably did have some kind of flu and should be home in bed. He could be running a high fever, she thought as she emerged from the Big Building into the soft air and pallid sunshine that had followed the extended rains.

She had never seen Felix in such a state. For her and for Joe, Felix had always been invulnerable, an unwavering source of strength. Others might fail or be found wanting, but never Jim Felix. His rise within the department had been almost spectacular and he had carried Joe with him. After Joe was killed, he had kept an eye on Norah. He had been and was still her sponsor, or in police parlance, her rabbi. Not that she didn't deserve her success, but she was honest enough to admit that it was Felix who had made it possible.

It was Jim Felix who had brought Norah to the attention of the C of D, Luis Deland. She had even been summoned to report to previous police commissioners, though not to the current PC, Peter Lundy. She owed Felix a lot, and the more she thought about it, the more concerned she became.

Should she mention the incident to Paula Lawson? Perhaps the secretary already knew, was concerned, but was doing nothing. Should she call Sally Felix? If the condition was the result of the antibiotics, then surely his wife knew about it. However, Sally might not know how severe his reaction was. Until she could find out what was going on, did she have any right to meddle?

Norah bought a hot dog from a street vendor and sat down on a wooden bench in the plaza to eat it.

It occurred to her that Felix's condition had distracted her from bringing up the reason for her visit. At least, Felix had not given any indication that she might be removed from the case. In fact, both he and Jacoby had urged her to clear the case quickly and get back to a normal routine. How did they expect her to do that alone, cut off from the privileges available to a police officer? Were they telling her to avail herself of the freedom and even license enjoyed by a private eye?

The idea of not having to justify every move was very appealing. Eagerly, Norah delved into her capacious pouch and found the folded square of paper Danny Neel had passed on to her. Next, she fished out her cell phone and called the top number on Danny's list. She waited for seven rings and was about to hang up, when a quavering voice answered.

"Yes?"

"Thomas Christie, please."

"He's not home. Who wants him?"

"This is Lieutenant Mulcahaney, Police Department, Fourth Division."

"Police?" The woman gasped.

"Is this Mrs. Christie?"

"Miss Christie. I'm his sister. What do you want with Tommy?"

"I just want to talk to him about a friend of his who died recently."

"You mean Bill? Bill Ciccerone?"

"You were acquainted with Sergeant Ciccerone?"

"Oh yes. He was a good man. A churchgoing man."

"Have you any idea why he might have killed himself?"

"The gates of heaven are barred to those who take their own lives. He knew that."

Her voice was taking on a strident edge, Norah thought. "I'm sure he did," she placated. "Did he appear worried or depressed recently? Did you notice a personality change?"

"He did miss the last couple of Saturday night poker games with his buddies. He'd never done that before. Tommy and the others were worried. I thought they made too much of it." The woman began to cry softly.

"Is there anywhere I can reach your brother, Miss Christie? A number where I can call him?"

"He's in the park at the Chess and Checkers Pavilion. There's some kind of exhibition or tournament . . . Bob Renquist is in it and Tommy went along. When you find him, tell him to come straight home. I need him." She ended in a high whine and hung up.

Norah put the portable phone away. She crossed Foley Square, entered the nearest subway station, and took the N train uptown to Fifth Avenue, exiting at Sixtieth Street. She crossed the street and entered the park at the south end of the zoo. Heading uptown, she passed the Delacorte clock, its storybook figures motionless till the next half hour. Using the underpass, Norah emerged within sight of the carousel and the Dairy on the other side. Just beyond was the chess and checkers area, which consisted of a small hexagonal structure very much like a hothouse. It was used in the winter. Today, of course, they were playing outdoors.

Norah counted twelve tables in a row. A man sat at each one, chessboard before him. They were a mixed group—some young, some old, and of various economic circumstances. Most were elderly, but there were more young people than she had expected—students from nearby Hunter College probably, she thought. Young or old, shabby or well dressed, every player was hunched over his board in fierce concentration. Meanwhile, the youngest of all, a boy still in his teens, slim in jeans and a camel hair blazer, strode up and down behind the empty chairs. He stopped briefly at each table, pondered the situation, made a countermove, and went on to the next.

A small but respectful crowd watched intently.

"Checkmate," the young master said to one of the seniors.

"Mate in two," he said to the next.

"That's Alexei Ivanov," Norah heard someone behind her whisper.

"The child prodigy?"

"He's only fifteen. Can you believe it?"

Within the next ten minutes young Ivanov finished off the rest of his opponents and received and acknowledged a modest round of applause.

The whole affair was very low-key, Norah thought as she scanned the spectators and participants, who had begun to disperse. A number of the latter stayed behind to study their boards to see where they had gone wrong. Norah approached the man in chair 10. His name was on the back: R. Renquist.

Her first impression was of a scholar: he had plenty of facial hair—beard, mustache, sideburns—and wore glasses. The impression was reinforced by his being here participating in a chess tournament. She approached him, her face open.

"Mr. Renquist? Congratulations. You gave him trouble."

"Not enough," Renquist replied. "But thanks." He reached for his cane, but when he had it she was still there. "Is there something I can do for you, Miss . . ."

"Lieutenant Mulcahaney, Homicide, Fourth Division. I'm looking for Thomas Christie. I was told he was with you."

Renquist's face didn't change; the cordiality remained, but he was wary. "Why do you want him?"

Norah had no idea how long Renquist had been retired, but his instincts were still sharp. She didn't know why, but that pleased her. So now she displayed her shield case. "I'm investigating Sergeant William Ciccerone's death."

Leaning heavily on his cane, Renquist struggled to his feet. As soon as he was steady, he reached out a scrawny hand and pumped Norah's hand with unexpected vigor. "I'm mighty glad to see you, Lieutenant Mulcahaney. I knew Bill didn't commit suicide. I knew it! I told the guys—no way Bill would do such a thing." He waved to a short, stocky man playing catch with a boy of about ten.

Christie made one last throw and then joined them.

"Tom Christie, Lieutenant Mulcahaney. She's investigating Bill's death," he informed his friend. "She heads up the Fourth."

"Overhead at Bill's precinct. Yes, I remember."

Christie was considerably younger than Renquist. He was clean-shaven and blessed with a full head of hair which he wore swept back from a high brow. His head was too large for his body, which made him look closer to the ground than he actually was. His features were sculpted on a bold scale. There were lines, but he was handsome in spite of them. Like Renquist, Tom Christie was very interested in what Norah had to say.

"I take it you know the circumstances of Sergeant Ciccerone's death."

Both nodded.

"But you don't believe he committed suicide."

"Bill and I went back more than twenty years," Renquist replied. "We were in the same class at the Academy. We double-dated. I know the man."

"He might have been under some unusual strain," Norah suggested.

"He was the most levelheaded, unflappable person you could ever meet."

"How about his health?"

"Never sick a day in his life."

"I heard he had a heart condition."

"He took medication for it. It was under control."

Norah persisted. "I was also told that he missed two of your regular Saturday night poker sessions because of a bad cold."

"Nobody kills himself because he has a cold."

Norah switched her attention to Christie. "Did you notice any change in your friend? Was he depressed? Anxious? Nervous in any way?"

Christie cast a pleading look at Renquist. Their eyes met. A decision was made.

"He did seem nervous," Christie admitted. "He kept looking over his shoulder like he thought somebody was following him."

Renquist jumped in. "He was on antibiotics for his cold. People get strange reactions from these drugs."

Apparently they'd had this discussion before, Norah thought. "Which is it going to be?"

They answered at the same time.

"Antibiotics."

"He was scared."

"How about both?" Norah asked. "That's possible, isn't it?"

Again the two men consulted without words and it fell to Renquist to explain.

"About a month ago, Bill started to behave oddly. We asked him what was wrong, but he wouldn't admit anything was amiss. We insisted and finally he told us he thought someone was stalking him. Someone was lurking around the house, he said. He was getting anonymous phone calls. They came only when he was home alone, so that meant whoever was making them had to be able to see his daughter and the girls coming and going. When Bill answered the phone he got only the dial tone or heavy breathing. Standard harassment, but it was obviously getting to him.

"The fact that the calls came only when he was in the house by himself indicated neither his daughter nor the grandchildren were targets and that was a relief, but he wasn't sleeping well. He had nightmares. He lost his appetite. We couldn't let him go on like that. We used to be cops, the two of us, along with Amos Hardeen and Greg Sommers . . ."

"I know."

"Okay. So we decided to find out exactly what was going on. We staked out the house and we tailed Bill. And we got nowhere. We bugged Bill's phone. Everything that came in or went out was normal and straight. Then Bill began to act queer. He talked to himself. Like I said, he kept looking over his shoulder as though he was being followed. He'd dart around corners or duck into a store like he was trying to shake the tail."

"Maybe he knew what you were doing and you were the ones he was trying to lose?"

Renquist blanched. "I never thought of that."

Norah scowled. "You should have reported this."

"We tried, Lieutenant. We were told nobody was available to take a statement. The squad was shorthanded, they said. So that was it. A couple of retired cops don't pull much weight."

Knowing she was responsible, Norah flushed. "Having been police officers yourselves, you know that can change not only from day to day but from hour to hour. You should have tried again."

"After a lot of agonizing, we decided against it. What we had to say would only strengthen the official line that Bill killed himself. We decided to believe Bill's version of what was happening to him. Now we know he was not hallucinating. Somebody was stalking him. That somebody killed him."

CHAPTER 11

▼ Murder.

From the beginning everything pointed to it. Up to now, no one had been willing to even voice the possibility, Norah thought. For a few moments she savored the satisfaction of having been right, but it didn't last. These two retired cops might support her, but their opinion wouldn't count for much. Still, she was encouraged.

"Sergeant Ciccerone did have a heart condition," Norah told Renquist and Christie. "His doctor was interviewed and confirmed it. No mention was made of a cold or flu, or that he was taking any medication other than heart pills."

"Like you said, Lieutenant, one doesn't preclude the other," Christie reminded her.

"Did your friend mention who he thought might be stalking him?" Norah asked. "We've all been threatened at one time or another by someone we've helped put away—empty threats usually, but sometimes . . . in this job, we make more enemies than friends."

Renquist shook his head. "He couldn't think of anyone, not even after going through his files."

"He kept files?"

"He was going to write a book. He had a bunch of notes and newspaper clippings, but they weren't organized in any way."

Like Stewart Schiff, Norah thought. Again she had to consider: Was she dealing with one crime and therefore with one perpetrator and five separate victims? Or with five separate crimes? One theory or the other had to be established as a starting point, and that meant going back to Stewart Schiff, maybe even farther to Foxworth and Kramer, the two Blue Deaths before him. That required manpower she couldn't have called up even in the best of circumstances. She thought longingly of the squad and the resources she might have had.

"Thank you, gentlemen. If you should think of anything else pertaining to the case . . ." She handed each of them one of her cards. "Use the home number. And once again, thanks."

They didn't let her get far.

"Lieutenant?" Renquist called after her.

She turned.

"We'd like to help." He was almost plaintive.

"You have already. More than you know." She waved and headed for the nearest park exit. On the way, she used her cellular to make sure the subject would be at home. She was, but she was less than enthusiastic at hearing from Norah.

"What's up, Lieutenant?"

"Nothing, really. I need to check a couple of things."

"Why doesn't that reassure me, Lieutenant?" Carol MacKenzie asked.

"I don't know," Norah replied. "I can be there in ten minutes."

Carol heaved a sigh. "I don't suppose I have a choice."

"In the final analysis, no, you don't." Norah pressed the button that cut the connection.

Carol MacKenzie must have been waiting at the door, because as soon as Norah rang she let her in.

"I'm sorry if this visit is inconvenient, Mrs. MacKenzie. I can come back at another time, if you prefer."

"It's as good as any. I'm sorry if I was rude."

"You're under a lot of strain. I understand."

"I've got fresh coffee brewing. Would you care for some?"

She didn't, but Norah didn't want to appear churlish in the face of Carol MacKenzie's attempt to be pleasant. "I never say no to freshly brewed coffee." Then she had to wait through the ceremony of serving it before she could get on with the questions.

"You did say your father had a bad cold and that he was taking medicine for it. Was it a prescription or over the counter?"

"I don't know."

"Would you mind if I took a look at his medicine cabinet?"

"What are you trying to prove?"

"I want to find out what happened to your father."

"He killed himself! That's what happened," she cried out. "He killed himself and left us destitute!"

Anger, one of the classic responses to the death of a loved one. "Why don't we go upstairs and have a look? Please, Mrs. MacKenzie." Surreptitiously, Norah looked at her watch. It was going on five; Mrs. Gantry was due to leave at six.

"You go on," Carol said.

"I'd prefer if you came with me."

"Whatever you want, Lieutenant. You're the boss." Carol set her cup down and stood. "This way."

Norah followed her up the stairs to the second floor.

The bathrooms were set back to back to accommodate the plumbing, of course. One was shared by Mrs. MacKenzie and the two girls. It was accessible by way of a small hall that linked the bedrooms. Panty hose and underwear hung on a line over the tub. The medicine cabinet was overstuffed with a variety of shampoos, bath lotions, and deodorants. A typically feminine accumulation.

"As I recall, the other bathroom opens off your father's room. Is that right?" Norah asked.

Carol nodded and again led the way. At her father's room she stepped to one side, inviting Norah to enter before her.

For a moment, Norah paused at the threshold. She had been here with Danny Neel—how many days ago was it? A profound change had taken place. The room wasn't the same. Norah believed that inanimate things were affected by events, just like people. When a family moved out of a house, for instance, and another family moved in, there was a palpable change in the atmosphere. A house that remained empty for a long time had a different aura from one that was filled with children.

On the day she and Danny were here, Cicerone's aura had been strong, dominant. Everything in the room had reflected it. It had been a cozy, Dickensian refuge from the modern world. No more. The room now was cold and impersonal. Norah walked around, stopping at this piece or that, touching, almost caressing.

The room had been thoroughly vacuumed and dusted, the heavy drapes taken down so that light poured in. The piles of books and papers that had given it so much of Ciccerone's spirit were all gone.

"It looks different."

"Thank you. Dad would never let me in here to give the place a really good cleaning. You can't imagine how much rubbish I had to get rid of."

Norah caught her breath. "His papers, his notes . . . You didn't throw anything away? Bills, receipts, documents . . ."

"I know better than that. I packed them in boxes to look over later."

"Why the rush, Mrs. MacKenzie? Your father's not buried yet."

Carol's face flamed scarlet. "I need to rent the room!" she exclaimed. "I need money to keep us going till I can sell the house. The insurance company doesn't pay off on suicides. All right? Not that it's any of your business."

"I'm sorry," Norah said. She had been insensitive and she regretted it, but she had to go on. "How about the bathroom? May I?" Without waiting, she walked over and opened the door. The place had been thoroughly scoured and polished, but all she was interested in was the medicine cabinet. It was small, but even so, there was plenty of empty space. There were four shelves. Starting at the top, the standard nostrums were neatly lined up: aspirin, Pepto-Bismol, something for gas relief, for diarrhea. Next shelf down: toothpaste, toothbrush, dental floss. Next, the larger items: cotton balls, rubbing alcohol, mouthwash, a man's hair dye. Ciccerone had still used shaving cream and a double-edged razor. Beside it was a four-ounce bottle of aftershave balm. No sign of any prescription medicine. Nothing for a cold except the aspirin.

"You haven't cleared this out," Norah remarked.

"I haven't got around to it."

"Where did your father keep his heart pills?"

"In the drawer of his night table."

Norah went back to the room and to the nightstand. Opening the top drawer, she immediately saw the plastic vial. The label taped to it read: *Coumadin: to be taken twice daily. Three refills.* It gave the doctor's name and was nearly half full. Norah pulled the drawer out the rest of the way and wedged in the back found a prayer booklet dedicated to the Infant of Prague and another to Saint Jude. There was a small packet of tissues. No other medication of any kind.

"How long had your father been taking the Coumadin?"

"A couple of years."

"And he showed no side effects?"

"To my knowledge, there are none."

"Had he changed dosage or switched medications?"

She shook her head. Danny Neel had asked that and also got a negative response.

"So as far as you know, he wasn't taking anything for his cold—prescription or over-the-counter?"

"I've already told you—no."

Why was she so resistant? "I'm sorry, Mrs. MacKenzie, I have to be sure."

"My father was extremely careful about possible interactions between drugs. He never took anything without first clearing it with his doctor."

Carol MacKenzie bowed her head and covered her eyes with her hands. She stayed that way for a while. The tears still quivered when she looked up again and continued. "He was sick. He wasn't himself. There were times when he didn't know me or the children." She took a deep breath. "He had Alzheimer's."

"Not everyone who has a memory loss or suffers periods of confusion and disorientation . . ."

"He had Alzheimer's," she repeated doggedly.

"Who told you that?"

"Anybody could see it."

"The one test to prove a patient has the disease can only be done after death. Did you know that?" Norah asked gently.

"No."

"That test was not performed as a routine part of your father's autopsy. There was no reason for it. But if you want it done, it's not too late."

"No! Leave him alone! I want you to leave him alone, that's all I want. I only said what I did because I thought maybe if I could convince you he was not responsible because of the disease, then maybe the insurance company would pay and I wouldn't have to sell the house . . ." She didn't try to hide the tears, but let them flow freely.

Norah put a hand on her shoulder. "Don't give up, Carol. It's not over yet."

▼ Norah hit the street right at the peak of the rush hour. She couldn't get a taxi. The buses were so crowded that when one finally came, she couldn't squeeze her way onto it. She started to walk. She alternately walked and ran across the park and then downtown to Sixty-eighth Street. She arrived home flushed and out of breath. And late.

"I'm sorry, Mrs. Gantry. Traffic . . . I'm very sorry."

"I'd appreciate it if you would call when you're going to be late, Lieutenant."

"I didn't intend to be late, Mrs. Gantry. I know you have other commitments and responsibilities and I respect them. It won't happen again."

"A simple telephone call to advise me how late you expect to be . . ."

"I'm sorry."

"Patrick didn't want to eat his supper because you weren't here."

"But he did finally eat?"

Relenting slightly, Ida Gantry smiled. "Yes, he did. He's a fine boy, Lieutenant. You're lucky. I wish I could stay with him full-time, but I can't."

At that moment, the door between the foyer and the corridor leading to the bedrooms opened and Patrick, in his pajamas, arms outflung, came running straight to Norah. She caught him up and hugged him.

"You're late, Mama. You're late!"

"I'm sorry, sweetheart."

"Mrs. Ida said nothing bad happened. She said you were all right."

"And I am, sweetie, I am." Norah hugged him again and put him down.

With the resilience of youth, Patrick skipped to another subject entirely. "The lady next door has a puppy. He's Chinese and he has a funny, wrinkled face. Could we have a puppy too?"

"We'll talk about it tomorrow, okay? Now it's back to bed."

She took the boy's hand in hers, waited till Mrs. Gantry let herself out and she heard the click of the lock as it fell into place, then walked Patrick back to his room. Together, they knelt at the side of the bed and recited:

> *"Now I lay me down to sleep,*
> *I pray the Lord my soul to keep;*
> *If I should die before I wake,*
> *I pray the Lord my soul to take."*

Then she helped him into bed, tucked him in, turned off the lamp but left the night-light on. Making sure the monitor was functioning, she bent over and kissed her son. He was already asleep. She left the room quietly, soothed and relaxed, at peace with herself and the world. Wandering into the kitchen, Norah found a note on the refrigerator door: *Two minutes in the microwave should do it. Ida.* On the center shelf inside was a macaroni and cheese casserole. It wasn't till after she'd consumed the last morsel that Norah thought to check her answering machine.

The red light blinked in groups of four, which meant there had been four calls, but when she pressed the message button the machine whirred, clicked, and whistled but no one spoke.

She hated when they did that.

▼ In the past few days, Jean-Marie Leclerc had gathered a considerable amount of information regarding Lieutenant Norah Mulcahaney. Now he was parked in a dusty Pontiac across the street from her building, watching. He saw the housekeeper leave. As daylight faded, a row of lights on the fifth floor came on: her apartment. He hadn't been tailing the woman long, but her habits were regular and he knew she was not likely to be going out again. Leclerc had no animus toward the woman detective, but she had a reputation for being meddlesome. With the most critical part of the job coming up, it might be wise to take her out. As a precaution.

In the midst of the years of violence in his country, the terrible brutality, the rape and theft and murder and torture, Jean-Marie had learned patience. He could, if need be, stalk a victim with the stealth of a jungle predator and lie in wait without food or water for long periods. But this case did not require that degree of effort.

It wasn't long before the lights on the fifth floor went out—all but one. He waited another twenty minutes to make sure she wasn't playing any tricks; then he turned on the engine and pulled out. He had other, more pressing concerns.

▼ Norah washed the dishes and set them on the rack to dry. She was restless. The sun had set, the sky darkened, and night enveloped the city. In the past this would not have been the end of the day's work. Now, because of Patrick, she couldn't go out. At this point in the case, she shouldn't need to. The legendary detectives solved their cases far from the scene, in solitude. Sherlock Holmes played his violin and, regrettably, smoked opium. Poirot used "the little gray cells." Nero Wolfe did his thinking while tending his orchids. Not that she put herself in their league, but fictional characters though they were, their methods were accepted and respected.

It was a matter of creating a relaxed atmosphere that would allow the subconscious to function freely. Norah had her own routine. She would put on nightgown, robe, and slippers, and lie down on the sofa—not in bed, where she might fall asleep. Comfortably settled, she would pick an aspect of the case which was particularly puzzling and conjure up every possible explanation, no matter how farfetched. She thought of it as solitary brainstorming.

By the investigation of possible motives in the Blue Deaths, Norah believed she had shown they were dealing not with suicide but with murder.

She had discovered the *why* of each death. She was now faced with the *how,* and that was more difficult.

Each man had put the barrel of his service revolver into his mouth and pulled the trigger. Simple if indeed he had done it himself, but not so simple if, as Norah believed, someone else had done it for him. The victim would most certainly have resisted—struggled, tried to save himself. To remain acquiescent meant he was unconscious. Say the perp was able to render the victim unconscious, whether by a blow to the head or by use of a drug, there was still the matter of the gun. In each instance, the victim was a cop and had been killed if not by his own hand, most certainly by his own gun. Of that there could be no doubt. It had been confirmed by examination of each of the fatal bullets under the comparison microscope.

Next problem: How did the perp come into possession of the victim's piece?

Norah got up and paced.

Outside the night deepened. She took a coffee break. Returning from the kitchen, she turned out the lights in the apartment, leaving on only her desk lamp. She sat down, leaned back in the chair, and picked up where she had left off.

Having rendered the victim unconscious, the perp took his gun from him. What other way was there?

Norah's breathing quickened; her heart pounded. Detectives Schiff and Douglas were on active duty and would certainly be carrying their pieces . . . but they had been killed in their own homes! Both of them. Would they have had their guns on them? Bill Ciccerone was retired. Undoubtedly, he had a permit to carry, but would he have had the gun on him when he was in his house alone? Yes, if he believed he was being stalked. Yes, if he was expecting a visitor, someone he feared.

How about the others, Schiff and Douglas? What reason might they have had to be armed at home? And if they weren't, the perp must have had a pretty good idea of where the weapon was kept. There were, after all, only so many places it was likely to be. It wasn't as though it was hidden and locked up.

If the time of death could be determined, that would help. With customary caution the assistant MEs so far had given only the standard two-hour spread. If none of them could do better, the detectives would try to pinpoint it through interrogation of neighbors and friends.

It was a big job. Multiply it by three and it was intimidating, but it wasn't the first time Norah had been faced with long odds. She wasn't fazed by the prospect of working alone. It only meant the job would take longer.

And she was still confronted with the original dilemma: Were these three killings—for the time being Norah excluded the Foxworth and Kramer deaths—committed by one perpetrator? She decided to go with the assumption that it was one perp.

Was he now satisfied? she asked herself. Or was there more to come?

And yet again, what was the connection between the victims?

She had asked herself that question over and over and found no answer. Well, now she had more avenues to explore. A week from Thursday Kevin Douglas would be buried with pomp and ceremony. She had at least till then. She picked up the phone and pressed the numbers she knew so well and waited for Phillip Worgan, Chief Medical Examiner of the City of New York, to answer.

CHAPTER 12

▼ "Damn!" Jim Felix winced as he nicked himself with the razor and again as he applied the iodine to the cut.

He felt lousy; there was no other word for it. His head throbbed. His hand was unsteady. He was by turns hot and cold. Probably running a fever. He should take his temperature, but if he did, Sally would fuss. She was watching him right now out of the corner of her eye. He decided to tell her straight out.

"I'm not feeling too well."

"Ah . . ." his wife sighed.

"I think I've got a cold coming on."

"We'll stay home."

"No, we won't."

"Why don't we take your temperature?"

"Because it's not necessary. I'm okay. I'll take a couple of aspirin, lie down for a while, and I'll be fine." To prove it, he got the aspirin bottle out of the bathroom medicine chest and shook two tablets into his palm, popped them into his mouth, and washed them down with half a glass of water. Perspiration glistened on his forehead. Abruptly, he sat down on the edge of the bed.

"I'm going to cancel," Sally Felix announced in a way that brooked no appeal.

"You can't. No, honey, please don't. I'll stay home, but you go. Please, darling."

His wife hesitated. A petite woman in her early fifties, her figure still trim, her red-gold hair shining, Sally Felix was a bundle of energy. Before marrying she had appeared on Broadway in small parts in shows that didn't last—critical successes that failed at the box office. She had fared better on television and had even been offered a role as a regular on a daytime soap opera. By then Felix had proposed and she had accepted. As the show was to be taped in Hollywood, it would have meant commuting between New York and L.A.—no way to start a marriage—and so she turned it down. She never regretted that decision, her only disappointment, and Felix's that they hadn't had children.

So Sally channeled her energies into working with underprivileged children. She got them interested in theater and the arts. She established the Five Boroughs Drama Workshop, which put on plays and involved the youngsters not only in acting but also in every aspect of production. These presentations were not sloppy amateur affairs, but professional and disciplined. She transmitted her own enthusiasm to the young adults, and the results were proof to those who supported the project that their money was being well spent.

A teenage scenic designer, for example, seeing his work translated from the drawing board to the three-dimensional, virtual reality of the stage, had little time left for drugs or hanging out with a gang. A girl, speaking the words of Juliet and hearing the audience applaud, would not be satisfied with the attentions of an inarticulate boyfriend; she would be less likely to have sex with him in some sleazy motel or in the back seat of a car. Over the years, chapters of the Drama Workshop had opened all over the country. Tonight, for her initiative, her dedication, and her determination, Sally Felix was to be honored at a dinner at the Waldorf-Astoria Hotel.

"I'm so proud of you, darling." Felix took her into his arms. "Either you go alone or I come with you, but I won't allow you to cancel. I can be just as stubborn as you." His smile shone with love.

"I don't like to leave you when you're sick."

"I'm not sick." There was just an edge to his denial. "Look, I'm going to take some hot tea and flop into bed. What are you going to do—stay home and watch me sleep? You're the guest of honor, Sally. You're going to disappoint a lot of people if you don't show." Shrewdly, Felix had made the appeal most likely to touch Sally—responsibility to others.

He followed up his advantage. "There'll be six hundred people in that ballroom waiting to applaud you. They will have come from all over the country—people you've worked with, children you've helped who are now grown up and leading good lives because of you." As he talked, Felix could see Sally's determination waver. "I tell you what—I'll take my temperature. If it's normal or close I'll come with you; over a hundred—I stay home and you go alone. Deal?"

▼ Sally went to the dinner alone and was uneasy all evening. She responded graciously to the praise and adulation and congratulations of friends and colleagues. She was touched by the effort that had gone into the affair, but her mind and heart were back with Jim. She could hardly wait for the evening to be over. However, she was scheduled to receive an award and give a short speech of acceptance, one she never would have gotten through had her remarks not been well rehearsed. As soon as she finished, she made her apologies to the event's chairman and slipped away.

The Broadway shows hadn't let out and the nightclubs hadn't opened their doors yet, so Sally had no trouble getting a cab. Traffic was light and she was back home in fifteen minutes. She paid the driver and was greeted by the night doorman, who escorted her across the lobby to the elevator. Everything seemed quiet and normal. Why should she think otherwise?

They lived on the eighteenth floor and it seemed to Sally Felix that the elevator had never been so slow. At last it stopped, the doors opened, and she stepped out into the quiet, softly lit hallway. By this time, in the face of so much that was normal, Sally's terrible anxiety had calmed somewhat. The shock, therefore, was all the greater when she put her key in the lock and discovered the door was already open.

Had she left it that way? No, impossible. Holding her breath, she eased the door open just enough so that she could see inside. The vestibule was lit only by the glow of a single, shaded lamp on the Chinese-style console. That was as it should be and she was reassured, though not completely. She eased the door a bit more, enough to slip inside.

It was very quiet. Both living room and dining room were dark. No light showed under the door of the master bedroom. Sally stood perfectly still and listened. There wasn't a sound, but somebody was there: she could sense a presence. A thief, of course. What should she do? Get out and go back downstairs and call 911 from the safety of the lobby? No. She didn't dare leave till she knew whether Jim was in danger. Most women kept their jewelry or other valuables in the bedroom, so the thief would have gone there first. Suppose Jim wakened? Coming out of a feverish sleep, what would he do? And how would the thief react?

These thoughts passed through Sally's mind with the swiftness of pulsars while at the same time she kept moving forward till she reached the bedroom. It too was dark, but there was enough light from the street for her to make out that Jim was sprawled on the bed.

"Jim?" she whispered.

He didn't answer.

Sally bent to him and whispered more urgently. "Jim?" Suddenly, she was aware of stealthy movement behind her. Before she could whirl around to face it, the darkness was shattered into starbursts of light.

▼ Sally Felix regained consciousness slowly. Bit by bit, she realized she was looking up at the small Austrian chandelier. So that meant she was lying on the floor. Somewhere a window was open and she shivered in the draft, goose pimples on her bare shoulders and arms. She was wearing a strapless ball gown. It took a while to remember why she was wearing it. While working on that, she became aware of Jim's foot hanging over the side of the bed—shoeless but with a sock. After that, everything came back fast. She scrambled to her feet and turned on the nearest lamp. What she saw shocked and frightened her.

The coverlet had been removed from the bed and neatly folded and placed on its rack, but the sheets had not been turned down. Jim was lying on top of them on his back. His narrow face was an unnatural ashen color and bloated. His mouth hung open and he was breathing with considerable difficulty. He was wearing the tuxedo pants and crisp, ruffled evening shirt he'd had on before she left.

His right arm was flung out and in his half-open palm his service revolver rested.

"Jim?" Sally cried aloud. "Jim, wake up. Please." She felt for his pulse but couldn't find it. She grasped his shoulders and shook him, but got no response. "Oh my God," she murmured. "Don't let this happen." Increasingly frightened, Sally tried to pull her husband into a sitting position in the hope of helping him breathe, but his dead weight was too much for her. Sobbing, she shook him some more. She slapped him—once, twice—and collapsed weeping on his chest.

He didn't stir.

▼ When the first RMPs arrived in answer to Sally Felix's belated but desperate phone call, Chief James Felix was alive but still unconscious. An EMS team arrived close on their heels. There were more RMPs and a second van. The cell phones crackled as instructions were issued from the control center and the technicians on the scene responded.

"He won't wake up! Why won't he wake up?" Sally tearfully appealed to the paramedic who seemed to be in charge. "What's the matter with him?"

Harvey Cole always made it a point to explain the situation to distraught family members if it was at all possible. On the occasions when he had no answers, he tried to let them down easy. "I'm sorry, ma'am, at this stage we can't tell. It could be for any number of reasons. I'm not a physician. We're taking him to the hospital. They're experts and they will surely find out."

In fact, at that moment, Jim Felix was being strapped to the gurney for transport.

"I want to go with him."

Harvey Cole looked her over and hesitated. She was on the verge of hysteria. "You're not in great shape yourself, ma'am. That's a nasty bump you've got on your head. You really should rest."

Sally gingerly touched the bandage they had insisted on putting on her head and winced. "I'm all right."

"You could have a concussion."

"I'm going with him."

Cole shrugged. "Don't you think you should change into something more . . . practical? You can catch up with the Chief at the hospital."

Suddenly, Sally was aware of how she must look—disheveled, her face tear-streaked, her mascara smudged, the lipstick chewed off. She looked down at her strapless gown slipping dangerously low. She might not care, but the paramedic was right—others would. Who could tell how long Jim would be in the hospital? There would be calls to make, errands to run. The gown was not merely inappropriate but cumbersome; she had already caught her heel in the hem and nearly tripped. She would feel better and function more efficiently in something other than a ball gown.

"Where will I find you? What hospital?"

"New York General. Go directly to the emergency room."

It was 11:02 on the Tuesday night when Sally Felix arrived home from the dinner at the Waldorf and found her husband comatose and was herself hit a glancing blow on the head. According to official records, her call to 911 was received exactly twenty-three minutes later, at 11:25. The first RMPs arrived in another three minutes and the first of the two EMS units were there seven minutes later—considered an excellent response time. When she reached the hospital, it took almost two hours of being shunted from one department to another before Sally was able to locate her husband, still strapped to the gurney in which he had been transported and parked in a side hallway.

She wanted a room for him.

"We haven't got a bed available, much less a room," she was told.

"I'll call my own doctor."

"Good idea. I wish you would," the resident replied with no animosity, only weariness. With his round, youthful face drawn, the former class prankster known for his sense of humor and his practical jokes no longer found much cause to smile. So Sally Felix did call her family doctor. Bernard Merlin was affiliated with New York General and had some clout there. After some diplomatic maneuvering over the telephone, Dr. Merlin was able to get his patient admitted. Ironically, the only available bed was in Neurology, which, as it turned out, was exactly where he belonged.

At last, Jim Felix was wheeled out of that side corridor. Sally attempted to accompany him, but was stopped. The doctors would be working on him, she was told; she could see him when they were through. She had to accept that. Once again Sally Felix found herself sitting on a bench with no idea where in that sprawling, labyrinthine maze they had taken her husband. There was nothing she could do but watch the hands of the clock on the wall as they swept round and round with interminable slowness. It was both quiet and dim in the waiting area, but she couldn't relax. One of the nurses offered her coffee, which she accepted gratefully. Nervous and tense as she was, a little caffeine wouldn't make much difference.

Dr. Merlin arrived at 2:32 A.M. He found Sally lying on her side on an imitation-leather couch. Her red-gold hair, loosed from the highly styled chignon she'd worn to the dinner, partially covered her face.

"Sally?"

She jerked awake.

"My dear." Merlin sat down beside her, took both her hands in his and held them. At sixty, Bernard Merlin was starting to think about retirement and was spending almost as much time on his boat as in his examining room. But he was of the old school, and though he was cutting down his patient list, he gave full attention and care to those he retained. Sally was one of these. She had been his patient long before she married Jim, and he became a patient because of her.

"What's happened?" Merlin asked.

"Jim wouldn't wake up," Sally moaned. "I tried everything. I shook him, slapped him. He didn't even flinch. Oh, Bernie, I didn't know what to do, so I called nine-one-one."

"You did exactly right. Have you any idea how Jim got into this condition?"

"He hasn't been feeling well these past few days. I had to go to a big benefit dinner. I wanted to cancel, but Jim wouldn't hear of it. So I went, but I couldn't shake this feeling that Jim was in trouble, so I left early. When I got home I found the front door open, I could sense somebody inside. I made my way to the bedroom in the dark, intending to take whoever it was by surprise, but before I could turn on a light, someone crept up behind me and hit me on the back of the head and I blacked out. When I came to, the intruder was gone and Jim was lying on the bed unconscious."

"Sally! My dear! How terrible for you. Are you all right now? Are you experiencing any pain? Double vision? Has anyone examined you?"

She drew back. "I'm fine. It's Jim who needs help. They won't tell me what's wrong with him, why he won't wake up."

"You said he wasn't feeling well. How do you mean? In what way?"

"I think he had the flu."

"Was he taking anything for it?"

She shook her head sadly. "A couple of aspirins. He said he was going to make himself a cup or tea, take another aspirin, and go to bed." As there was no comment from Merlin, Sally went on. "You know Jim. He's leery of medicine. Getting him to take an aspirin is a major achievement."

Merlin patted her hand. "Let's see what I can find out."

She watched as Merlin passed through the swinging doors at the end of the corridor, where she'd been stopped. She felt better now that someone who knew them was taking charge. She got herself more coffee from the vending machine, and as she sipped it she paced and watched the clock. Ten minutes, half an hour, an hour. The minutes dragged.

When they were first married, Sally, like so many police wives, worried every morning when Jim went to work whether she would see him again that night. Would he return to her unharmed? There had been some close calls: shoot-outs, a high-speed car chase in which Jim had broken a leg. But as the years passed and he rose in rank and took on duties that were mainly administrative, she began to relax. Jim followed a regular schedule, almost like a civilian, and she hardly thought about the dangers of the job except when a cop was killed. Now this! *Dear God,* she prayed, *let him be all right!*

Feeling a hand on her shoulder, she jumped.

"Sorry to startle you." It was Bernard Merlin.

"Is Jim awake yet? Did you find out what's wrong with him?"

"No. They don't know yet. They've done some tests, but the results are not conclusive. They'll do some more tomorrow. Well, it's already tomorrow, isn't it?" He tried a smile, but Sally didn't respond.

"He shows no indication of physical trauma—no blow to the head, for example, that might account for his condition. The next tests will be to identify the presence of the most common drugs."

"You know that Jim doesn't use drugs," she protested.

"They have to start somewhere. It would help if we had an idea what to look for." It was actually a question which she didn't choose to answer. Merlin didn't give up. "The most mystifying thing is the gun. You didn't mention the gun, Sally."

"I don't remember any gun."

"The patrol officer who came in response to your nine-one-one call reported that Jim was lying on the bed unconscious and with a gun in his hand."

Sally shook her head, bewildered. "Jim carries his gun when he's on duty, of course. But at home? I've never seen it. I don't know what he does with it."

Merlin sighed. "At least the gun hasn't been fired recently."

"He was hardly in a condition to shoot," she pointed out tersely. Then her eyes narrowed. "Why are you asking me these questions? You sound like you think Jim's done something wrong."

"No. Of course I don't. The police . . ."

"The police appear to have forgotten who James Felix is." Her eyes threw off sparks. "I'll remind them."

"Let me take you home, Sally." Bernard Merlin picked up her jacket and held it for her to slip into.

But she took a step back. "I'm not leaving."

"You'll do no good here. You can't help Jim. You'll exhaust yourself for nothing."

"It won't be for nothing if he wakes up. Suppose he wakes and there's nobody with him? Suppose he can't remember what happened? How will he feel?"

Merlin didn't want to tell her that there was little likelihood of Jim Felix's regaining consciousness anytime soon.

"I want to be right beside his bed so that I'll be the first person he sees."

"I'm afraid you can't do that. There's another patient sharing the room."

"Can't you get him a private room?"

"Not tonight. Anyway, he's better off sharing. He'll get twice the supervision."

"May I see him?"

"Of course," Merlin answered promptly, glad he could accommodate her in something. "He's in room four-oh-seven. This way."

So Sally learned where they had put her husband.

It was almost four A.M.

She spent the next four hours in the waiting room adjacent to Felix's room, twisting and turning on the stiff, unyielding couch, trying to sleep. She dozed awhile, got up and paced, peered into Jim's room now and then. He remained silent and inert. His roommate, however, snored loudly and regularly. All that Sally could see of him was his stomach—a mountain of pink flesh showing through the spaces between the buttons of his pajama top.

At seven-thirty A.M., the hospital's rhythm began to change as the night shift prepared to go off and the day staff to come on. Sally woke on her sofa not remembering when she had returned to it. Stiff, groggy, disoriented, she found her way to the ladies' room, washed her face and combed her hair. She was glad she had followed the paramedic's advice last night and changed out of her ball gown. She made herself as presentable as she could and then returned to room 407. The door was half open. She walked right in.

It seemed to Sally Felix that her husband was exactly as he had been when she'd left him a few short hours ago, and seeing him like this—supine and helpless, tubes sprouting from nostrils and veins, ugly purple bruises on his arms at the points of entry, connected by patches taped to his chest to a machine that showed his vital signs on a screen—made her want to cry. She bent her head close to his and whispered to him.

"Who did this to you, darling? Who was it? Wake up and tell me. Please, Jim, wake up."

Suddenly, it struck Sally Felix that she had resources most citizens did not. Her husband held a high position in the police department. He was the right hand of Chief of Detectives Luis Deland. She could call Deland and he would come.

In fact, Luis Deland was already there, striding down the hall with an aide at each side like a general come to inspect the troops. Deland was a tough cop of the old school with a weather-beaten, creased face and an unlit cigar usually protruding from the side of his mouth. In deference to hospital regulations, the Chief had discarded the cigar. He would replace it as soon as he left the building. Once in his own chauffeured car, he might even light up.

"Sally!" he exclaimed, and striding to her, swallowed her in an embrace. "How is he?"

"Oh, Luis, I don't know. He won't wake up. I don't know how he got this way. Our own doctor was here last night . . . this morning. He says Jim might have taken medicine for his cold and it interacted with something. But what? Jim doesn't drink or smoke. He doesn't dose himself."

"Don't worry, we'll find out. What we need to know from you is why Jim was carrying his piece in the house last night."

"I don't know. I didn't see it. He didn't mention it. Why is everybody worrying about the gun?"

"It doesn't fit the rest of the pattern, Sally. We can't ignore it. But you leave it to me. You've been here all night; you must be exhausted. I'll have one of my men take you home. Do you have anyone staying with you?"

"I'm not leaving here. I'm not leaving Jim. As long as he's here, I stay."

"Be reasonable."

"This is a big hospital. It's well staffed, plenty of doctors and nurses and all kinds of technicians and orderlies and so on, but there's nobody that can sit with my Jim and watch over him and only him. I can do that. And that is what I'm going to do."

CHAPTER 13

▼ Norah heard about it over the radio on the eight A.M. news. She rushed to the television and was just in time to catch a shot of C of D Luis Deland, flanked by two aides, stopping at the door of room 407 to embrace Sally Felix. The commentator paused for the close-up and then continued.

"James Felix, a three star chief, is CEO for Luis Deland, head of all NYPD detectives. Felix was scheduled to escort his wife, Sally, known for her work with juveniles through the Drama Workshop, to a dinner in her honor last night. He complained of feeling unwell and stayed home while she went on. Mrs. Felix returned early to find him unconscious. All attempts to rouse him have failed. Mrs. Felix has refused to leave her husband's side till he regains consciousness. . . ."

Poor Sally, Norah thought. The glimpse she'd got of her on the TV wasn't encouraging. How could she help? No use trying to call the hospital; their switchboard would be swamped. She could go over herself—Mrs. Gantry was due at any moment. While she waited, Norah called the Felixes' housekeeper and asked her to pack an overnight bag for Mrs. Felix. Norah would pick it up on the way.

Norah was familiar with New York General and could find her way through its labyrinth of corridors. But when she got to Felix's room, he wasn't there. One bed was stripped down; the other was occupied by an obese man of indeterminate age who was greedily wolfing down the meager food on his tray.

"Excuse me, sir. I understood there was another patient in this room."

"Right. They took him away."

"What?"

"They transferred him to better accommodations. He's in the Tower Suites." He eyes Norah hopefully. "You wouldn't happen to have a candy bar on you, would you?"

"I'm sorry."

"Or a mint, or anything?"

"Sorry," Norah said, and fled.

Following directions of the floor nurse, Norah located the bank of elevators servicing the exclusive Tower Suites and took the nearest to the top floor. She stepped out to a small rotunda from which three spokes emanated, each one leading to a single, separate suite. The entire area was carpeted, temperature controlled, and lulled by soft music. A brass wall plaque pointed the way to Suite C. A uniformed officer stopped her at the door.

Courtesy of Chief Deland, Norah thought. Though the guard was suitably impressed when she produced her credentials, he insisted on examining the contents of the small valise. As he should, she thought. Satisfied that everything was as she had represented, the guard stepped aside and she went in.

Ignoring the panoramic view of the East River and the steely grandeur of its bridges, hardly registering the luxurious appointments, though she was to admire them later, Norah went straight to Sally Felix, who was hunched over in a corner, her head in her hands.

Norah cleared her throat. "Sally . . ."

Silently, they clung to each other. After a few moments, they separated.

"What happened?" Norah asked while studying her friend. "I heard on the news it was a stroke."

"I don't know. The doctors don't say. They think it might be an allergic reaction to medication he was taking for a cold. But he wasn't taking anything," she wailed. "They've scheduled more tests."

"They'll find out what it is and they'll fix it," Norah assured her. "This is one of the finest hospitals in the world. Here." She handed the small valise to Sally. "I stopped by your house and picked up a few things for you just in case . . . but probably you'll be going home soon and won't need them."

"Norah, I'm afraid he'll never wake up."

"Don't say that. Don't think it." Once again, the women embraced. "May I see him?"

"Of course."

From the elegant anteroom they passed to a standard hospital room with no pretense of being anything else. The patient lay on a standard hospital bed with the usual monitors and machines surrounding him. Norah picked her way to Jim Felix's side. She thought she was prepared, but she wasn't—not for this, not to see Jim Felix, with his lion's mane of hair, his piercing green eyes, his strong jaw, reduced to an inert mass with a machine breathing for him. Aware that Sally was behind her, waiting intently for her reaction, Norah tried to find a middle response between her own shock and the need to give hope to her friend. Words were not adequate. Action was required.

"Does anybody know how this happened? Does anybody have any idea how it happened?"

Sally pulled a tissue from her handbag, wiped her eyes and blew her nose. "They tell me that the initial report states Jim was found lying on the bed unconscious and that he had a gun in his hand. I didn't see any gun. At least, I don't remember seeing one. I was too upset worrying about whether he was dead or alive."

Good, Norah thought. She was calming down. "Of course, but what about earlier in the evening, before you left for the dinner? Did he have the gun out then?"

"He might have. I don't know. I wasn't thinking about guns. Why is everybody so worked up about it? He was probably putting it away for the night just as the intruder broke in . . ." She couldn't finish.

Norah let her work through it alone. Sometimes too much sympathy made it harder. When it seemed Sally had herself in hand, she went on. "Where does Jim usually keep his service revolver when he's home?"

"He has a small safe at the back of his closet, but he seldom bothers to put it there. Mostly he just tosses it into a bureau drawer."

Where he could easily get ahold of it if necessary. "Could he have been expecting to meet someone later on?"

"I don't know."

"Could he have used the cold as an excuse to get you out of the house?"

Sally gasped. "Jim wouldn't lie to me. Or risk involving me in any police business. You know better than that!"

In fact, Norah knew that Jim Felix was obsessive about keeping the job and home apart. Also, she felt odd discussing Jim as though he wasn't there. She wondered how much of what was going on and being said reached him through the layers of unconsciousness.

"Why don't we go into the other room and sit down together and see if we can't make heads or tails out of this. I noticed a small kitchen. There must be coffee or tea . . ."

"Stop treating me like an invalid, Norah," Sally Felix cried out suddenly. "You, all of you, including Chief Deland, are tiptoeing around me like you're walking through a minefield. You want me to be straight with you, but you're not straight with me."

"We're still trying to sort things out. We still don't have all the facts, Sally." Though she hadn't spoken to the C of D, or to anyone officially on the case, Norah felt safe in taking a stand. "You've told me what the situation was before you left for the Waldorf. Now tell me what happened when you came home."

Sally sniffed. She fumbled for a tissue. Norah produced one from her pouch and handed it to her.

"All through that evening I had an intuition that something bad was going to happen. I couldn't wait to get away. When I entered the lobby, everything seemed normal. By the time I got upstairs, I was almost reassured; then I put my key in the lock and discovered the door was open. When I got inside, things were quiet and so again I convinced myself that everything was all right and the open door was due to my own carelessness. So I stepped inside and I was just about to turn on the lights when I heard a noise, a kind of thud, in the bedroom. I called out to Jim, but he didn't answer.

"By then I was sure my first instinct had been right—there was somebody in the apartment, an intruder, a thief."

"Did you turn on the lights?"

"No. I was afraid if I turned them on and got a look at him, he'd have to kill me."

She was right, Norah thought.

"Anyway, the intruder made the decision for me." Sally ruefully rubbed the bump on her head where the bandage had been.

"Where was Jim while this was going on?"

"On the bed. He hadn't moved."

"You told this to the detectives?"

Sally nodded. "And to Chief Deland."

"And what was their reaction?"

"They said probably the perpetrator was as anxious to get away as I was to have him get away. They wanted to know what he had taken. I hadn't looked. It was the last thing on my mind."

"Understandably, but it might be a way to trace the perp. Through the stolen goods," Norah elucidated. "Well, we won't worry about that now. When he wakes up, Jim will tell us exactly what occurred."

"Do you really think he'll come out of this?"

"I haven't a doubt in the world," Norah lied, convincingly, she hoped.

"Then why did Chief Deland put a guard on the door?"

It took a few moments for Norah to come up with an answer. "To keep the media out of your hair."

Sally Felix didn't believe it. Norah herself didn't. Luis Deland would not have put a police guard on the door of the suite just to stave off intrusive reporters. There had been an attempt on Deland's right-hand man to put him to sleep permanently. The C of D, Norah thought, was trying to thwart a second attempt.

▼ Norah could hardly wait to contact Chief Deland. She took the express elevator down to the ground floor and exited into a small garden. She found a secluded place to sit and pressed Deland's number on her cellular, her eagerness growing with every ring. At last, the Chief's secretary picked up.

"Miss Lasker? This is Lieutenant Mulcahaney. May I speak to Chief Deland, please?"

"I'm sorry. He's in a meeting."

"When do you think it'll be over?"

"I have no idea, Lieutenant, but directly after, he has an appointment with the PC. I don't know how long that will last." Her tone was cool as a mountain brook, but not refreshing.

Norah knew Ruth Lasker to be a very attractive woman. She had abundant chestnut hair, flawless skin, large brown eyes. She dressed with style and kept herself meticulously groomed. She was a skilled secretary.

"Didn't you have enough time with him at the hospital this morning?"

Norah was shocked at the naked envy.

"This is new information," she explained.

"If you care to leave a message—" Ruth Lasker began, and stopped. Her tone changed subtly. "Tell me what you have, Lieutenant. I'll pass it on to the Chief."

"I can't do that." Norah was curt. She didn't have time for this kind of maneuvering. "It's too complicated." That wouldn't sit well. In trying to smooth over the situation, she had made it worse. "I'm sorry. What I mean is—"

"Do you want to leave a message, or don't you, Lieutenant? I have calls waiting."

It knocked the breath out of Norah. Never before had she been denied access to the Chief. She realized that the manner in which this was resolved would provide the guideline for the future. "Tell the Chief, when you have a chance, naturally—don't interrupt whatever it is he's doing—tell him I have a new lead with regard to the attack on Chief Felix. He knows where to reach me." With that she clicked off. It now depended on the extent of the secretary's resentment. Would she risk delaying the message? The ring of the cellular was her answer.

"What's on your mind, Norah?"

It was Deland himself. A skirmish won, but there was no time to savor it. "Sir, I think Chief Felix is being drugged. I believe he's been under the influence for a considerable period."

There was a pause, a very long pause. When he spoke again, Deland's tone could only be described as black.

"Where did you get an idea like that?"

She must not allow herself to be intimidated, Norah thought. "His demeanor. I spoke with him in his office on the morning before this incident. He was not himself. He said he had a bad cold. In fact, Sergeant Ciccerone's behavior before his death was similar to the Chief's and he told his friends he had a bad cold. In fact," Norah exclaimed with a flash of insight, "each of the victims exhibited similar symptoms."

"Explain that, Lieutenant."

"I think the buildup of the drug in the bodies of the intended victims reached the point where they were rendered close to comatose. In the Chief's case, that occurred on the night of Mrs. Felix's dinner. The perp expected it and was lying in wait. He saw her leave and waited awhile to make sure everything was quiet upstairs, and then went in. He discovered Chief Felix passed out on the bed. He located the Chief's gun, placed it in his hand, and was just about to position it in the Chief's mouth when he was interrupted.

"Sally Felix interrupted him. By coming home early, Sally saved her husband's life." Norah paused.

Through a series of grunts and throat clearings, she could visualize the tough old cop chomping thoughtfully on his cigar.

"How did the perp gain access? How did he know Sally Felix would be going out that particular night? How did he know where to find Jim's service revolver?" Deland challenged. "Too many holes, Lieutenant."

"The Waldorf affair and Sally Felix's part in it have been highly publicized," Norah pointed out. "The rest can be explained too. We haven't even started on this lead."

Another pause, then a decision.

"It's much too iffy. Forget about it, Lieutenant. The doctors tell me Jim's condition is due to a stroke. When he comes out of it, he'll tell us everything."

"Excuse me, sir, when will that be?"

"Nobody can tell. Could be days or weeks. Let's hope it's days. Meantime, what's your situation at home?"

He sounded friendly, almost like the old days. "I'm clear for weekdays but no nights or weekends yet."

"Well, straighten yourself out and let us know."

"Yes, sir, I'll do my best."

"Don't wait too long."

"No, sir. Thank you, sir."

The last stuck in Norah's throat, but it didn't matter, the Chief of Detectives had already hung up. She stared at the phone in her hand and shut it off. The message couldn't have been clearer: She could go back *on their terms.* Otherwise, she wasn't wanted or needed.

She had sprung her theory on Deland too soon, Norah decided. She should have had a better basis for her allegations, but she had allowed herself to get carried away by what was at best only a theory. Actually, Deland hadn't suspended her as she had halfway expected. He hadn't ordered her off the case. Should she read the failure to do so as support? That would be stretching optimism. Producing a small notebook from that well-stocked pouch, Norah found Bob Renquist's telephone number and reactivated the cellular. The retired cop answered on the second ring.

"Lieutenant Mulcahaney! What a pleasant surprise. What can I do for you?"

"You said earlier that you would like to help find Bill Cicerone's killer."

"That's right."

"Does the offer still stand?"

"You bet."

Norah was gratified both by the prompt response and by its intensity. "Would it be possible for you to come to my home at, say, seven tonight?"

"The four of us?"

"If the others are willing."

"They'd never forgive me if they were left out."

▼ As she prepared for the meeting, Norah was reminded that the men she was enlisting were volunteers and as such had to be handled carefully. On the other hand, they had been cops and so should not flinch at certain assignments that might put a civilian off. They would not complain about the monotony of surveillance, and would be very careful about how they handled evidence. This last was by no means guaranteed. Despite the sophistication of modern forensics, plenty of cops and even detectives contaminated a crime scene, whether through ignorance or laziness. Norah had a hunch that Renquist and company, though they might not be in on the latest methods, would not be guilty of carelessness.

They arrived in a group promptly at seven. After cordial introductions—Norah had not met Sommers and Hardeen—she showed them into the living room. As each man took his place and settled himself, he brought out a notebook and pen. Norah smiled to herself. Procedure required every officer under the rank of captain to carry a notebook and write down all the facts of a case. The act was the signal that though they were volunteers, they knew what to do. In response, Norah brought out her own daily diary.

"First of all, I want to thank you for coming," she began. "I also want to tell you why I've asked you here, and finally, explain my personal situation."

Norah had made what was in essence the same speech to Wyler, Neel, and Ochs. She paused for a moment to scrutinize their replacements and was not encouraged. These men had been street cops, rough and tough, and it still showed. But age had smoothed the sharp edges and that was the crux of her unease: they were old. Old cops. Renquist she had already pegged as past seventy; Christie had to be early sixties; and Gregg Sommers, tall and skinny, his dark coarse hair cut in the trendy style called a flattop, and dressed "young" in jeans and a nice blazer, had to be close to sixty himself. Amos Hardeen, "the kid," barely cleared fifty, but he was in a wheelchair. What had she gotten herself into?

"Naturally, we're curious to know why you need us." Renquist assumed the role of spokesman, which was evidently his custom. "I checked you out, Lieutenant. You've got a big job and a big reputation. So why are you here instead of in your office? Why do you want to work with a bunch of has-beens?"

Norah flushed. She was tempted to call the whole thing off. How could she do it without offending them?

"Take it easy, Bob," Christie chided. "The lieutenant doesn't have to tell us anything."

"Yes, I do," Norah said. "When we talked in the park, you told me Sergeant Ciccerone claimed he was being stalked. You took turns tailing him without result. Meanwhile, he continued to show signs of instability: he talked to himself, he kept looking over his shoulder. You didn't know that he'd seen you until one day he shook off the tail."

"We were trying to protect him," Hardeen explained.

"Of course you were." She nodded. "I'm sure you've heard that

Chief Felix is in a coma." She took time to look at each man in turn. "So far we have no idea how he got that way or how long it will be till he comes out of it. It strikes me, however, and I think you'll agree, that there's a similarity here. Bill Ciccerone had a bad cold verging on the flu, but when I went through his medicine cabinet yesterday afternoon, I found no cold medicine of any kind. Chief Felix also had flulike symptoms. He is known to avoid any kind of patent or prescription medicine. He went to bed early last night and hasn't wakened since. One man is dead; the other may never wake up."

She was met with shocked silence.

Norah continued. "I am on extended leave. I don't want to be but my personal situation requires it. I don't know when I'll be able to get back to the precinct. Meantime, my theory isn't getting much credence." She sighed and her chin dropped slightly. "I can't allow my people to take on the burden of trying to prove it by working on their own time, but I do need help."

She stopped, took a deep breath, and waited for the response.

It took a while coming. Amos Hardeen in the wheelchair asked the hard question. "What do you think happened, Loo?"

"Both cases were to appear to be suicides. They were staged to look like each man had turned his own gun on himself. In order to set it up, each victim had first to be rendered unconscious. Your friend's hallucinations, his sense of being followed, talking to someone who wasn't there, had to be drug-induced. Chief Felix's symptoms—high fever, chills, tremors—are also symptomatic of certain drugs and are subject to being misinterpreted as flu."

"God!" Amos Hardeen gasped.

"Did your friend still have his revolver?" Norah asked, because not all retired officers did.

"Bill had a license to carry, but he didn't make use of it till recently. There was one time . . . in the park . . . You remember?" He appealed to Renquist.

"A poor black guy was sitting on a park bench. He was muttering to himself but not bothering anybody. Suddenly, out of nowhere,

Bill comes charging down the path, points his gun at the bum and orders him out. The guy ran, rags flapping in the wind. He didn't stop till he was out in the street and dodging traffic."

"Then there was the housewife coming out of the supermarket," Christie recalled.

Each one, it seemed, had a story.

"Bill tried to arrest her as a prostitute. She screamed and dropped her groceries on the sidewalk. We had to hustle him away before a squad car showed up. It wasn't easy to placate her either. She wanted to sue the department, anybody."

"It must have been very sad for you to see your friend go downhill like that. But suppose what he claimed was true? Suppose he *was* being stalked. Somebody could have been out to get him. We make more enemies than friends in this job."

No one had an answer. Renquist, however, had a question. "How do you explain the incidents we've just described?"

"Those are some of the things we need to find out." She was pleased. These men were not dummies. "I believe that the perp fed the drug to his intended victim gradually. The effect was cumulative. He was familiar with it and knew what to expect. At a certain stage and when he knew the victim to be alone—he went in. He set the scene and caused his puppet to carry out the script."

"Well then, if the same thing happened to Chief Felix, he'll be able to tell us everything when he wakes up."

"I think we'd better not wait."

With one sweeping glance, Bob Renquist polled his friends. Then he turned to Norah. "What do you want us to do, Lieutenant?"

"I'm told that Sergeant Ciccerone was thinking of writing a book. I assume it was to be about the Job and the cases he worked on. His daughter has stashed his notes and papers in their basement. I'd like two of you to go through them. Make a list case by case of everyone involved: the accused, lawyers, witnesses, court personnel, police. You know what's needed. If the same name shows up on more than one list, we may have something. It's a tedious job, I know," she apologized.

"Right up my alley, Lieutenant," Hardeen assured her.

"We used to be partners," Greg Sommers told her. "It would be good to work together again."

"All right." Norah nodded. "Bob, I'd like you to canvass Sergeant Ciccerone's neighborhood. Find out if anyone observed a stranger loitering. If the murder was committed as I've described, then the perp had to watch his victim closely. He not only had to know to what extent the drug was proving effective but also had to know the victim's routine and that of his family. Okay?"

"You've got it, Lieutenant."

"You'll work with him, Mr. Christie?"

"Call me Tom."

"I'm Norah." With that the alliance moved up a level.

"We need to examine Chief Felix's records," she continued. "I believe Mrs. Felix will permit me to look over any documents the Chief has at home. The records in his office of course are something else. If he were conscious, we wouldn't need to ask."

CHAPTER 14

▼ Everything had been done according to ritual, Jean-Marie Leclerc thought as he sat in the room he had been renting for the past six months and which he hoped he would be vacating soon. The furnishings were minimal—a narrow cot, a scarred bureau, an off-balance table, and a couple of chrome-legged chairs. A washbasin was hidden behind a screen; shower and john were down the hall. The only item of value was the computer. Leclerc lived in austerity, but his computer and its appurtenances were top-of-the-line. He saw nothing incongruous in the union of ancient beliefs and modern miracles. He was surfing the Internet in search of an ad he'd noticed a while back. He hadn't been interested then, but had stored the information in the back of his mind for later if needed. The conjure was still holding, but for how long? At that moment, the information he'd been seeking appeared on the screen.

WANT TO CAST A SPELL?
The Nine African Powers Shop in New Orleans, LA, can help you. We offer the best voodoo doll service. We have in stock black, red, and green dolls. Undressed $3, Dressed $6. When ordering send person's name, a piece of their hair and clothing, or a picture. You need one doll for each person. Spell works

faster with the personal items belonging to the person the doll represents attached to the doll. In casting the spell, stick doll with a pin while talking to it.

Not a problem, Leclerc thought. While the hospital room remained under police guard, Felix's apartment did not. He could enter it at will. But he shouldn't have to. He had done everything right. It wasn't his fault that the victim's wife had come home sooner than she was supposed to.

▼ The days dragged by and Jim Felix's condition remained the same. *Stable,* the hospital said whenever Norah called. Sally Felix continued to keep vigil at his bedside, occupying the guest room of the suite at night.

Norah dropped in at least once a day. It seemed to her that Felix was slipping deeper and deeper into the netherworld. He was totally unaware of their presence. They spoke to him, but he didn't hear. He no longer reacted to music or to the touch of Sally's lips on his.

It was Norah's belief that a problem was best solved by direct action. Ask and you're likely to receive. So she asked Sally straight out for permission to examine the papers the Chief kept at home.

Sally agreed readily. The ordeal of waiting was taking its toll on her, but for a moment a light flared in her tired eyes.

"It's a long shot," Norah warned her.

"As long as there's a chance, any chance. You do what you have to do."

Unfortunately, Jim Felix was not the kind to bring work home, since he made every effort to keep the evil he dealt with every day from touching Sally. He had an elegant paneled study, with floor-to-ceiling bookcases, a comfortable desk, and a nicely camouflaged file cabinet. Norah had the keys Sally had given her, but found only personal correspondence and bills. She went through them, but though she had permission, she couldn't help but feel she was intruding. And she found nothing, only the keys to Felix's office on a separate ring, tagged and lying in the center drawer of the desk almost as though he wanted them found, which of course, was ridiculous. Nevertheless, she picked them up and put them in her handbag. Using them was something else.

Before leaving, Norah took a look at the bedroom. It had already been cleaned, naturally, and before that it had been thoroughly searched. Norah knew she was no match for the team that had conducted the "toss," but there was always the chance, the possibility, that something had been overlooked. She stood on the threshold and the hunch came to her to try to see what the perpetrator had seen. To do that, she turned out the lights. When her eyes became adjusted to the change, she saw that the illumination from the street was considerable and focused on the bed where Jim had been lying unconscious. Now all the perp had to do was locate Jim's gun. Whether he looked there first or last, he found it in the nightstand on what Norah assumed was Jim's side of the bed.

▼ Norah Mulcahaney had always abided by the rules. That was the way her widowed father had brought her and her two brothers up. That training was reinforced when she joined the department and again when she married Joe. Not that she was averse to setting a trap for a criminal. She had not only concocted but also participated in some effective stings. But that was only after every other possibility had been explored and found inadequate. She had yet to ask for Chief Deland's help. Jim Felix had always been there to do it for her.

"Chief Deland is not available," Ruth Lasker pronounced, clearly no mellower since their last exchange. If anything, the civilian secretary was more truculent.

"Where can I reach him? It's important."

"Every call is important." Lasker's tone implied Norah's was well at the bottom of the list.

"Of course." Norah got the message but ignored it. "When do you expect him back?"

"Not till next week. He's in Miami attending a meeting of police chiefs."

Norah was momentarily dismayed. "He'll be calling in, I suppose. May I leave a message?"

"What's the message?"

There was no way Norah could convey the urgency of the situation to this woman, as she had only recently started working for the C of D. She had no understanding of her boss's background, or of the relationship between him, Jim Felix, and Norah herself. Or maybe she did and that was the cause of her resentment. In the early days when women were fighting for a toehold in the department, they had stuck together and formed a solid front. Now, having gained so much, the ranks were breaking up. Instead of being proud of each other's accomplishments, they were jealous.

"What shall I tell Chief Deland?" Lasker pressed.

"Just say I called, and ask him to get back to me as soon as possible."

"He's a very busy man. If you could give me some idea . . ."

"I'll wait till I can talk to him."

"Up to you, Lieutenant," Lasker snapped, and hung up.

That hadn't helped matters, Norah thought as she too hung up. She could call Miami and trace the Chief easily enough. That would be going over Lasker's head and Deland wouldn't be pleased; she knew him well enough to be sure of that. So she was left with no choice but to go through the files in Jim Felix's office. The very thought sent chills through her. On the other hand, how long could she wait? With each day that passed, Felix's hold on life became weaker. How long did she dare wait?

If she was going to do it, then she should do it *now*. However, it wasn't all that simple. There were four keys on the ring she had found in Jim's desk at home: two were for Segal locks, probably for the entrance door and for his private office; the two smaller ones would be for his desk and files, just like at home. Getting into the building was no problem. Once in, she would wait till the executive offices shut down and then make her move.

She had forgotten one thing: Who would be home with Patrick?

▼ "I know I promised not to ask you to work extra hours, Mrs. Gantry, but this is a very crucial situation."

"It's all right, Lieutenant, I understand."

"I can't turn this job over to anybody else." Though Mrs. Gantry had already agreed, Norah was geared to make her pitch and continued. "I can't even guess how long the job will take."

Since starting to work for Norah, Ida Gantry had learned a lot about her employer from neighbors in the building, from newspapers, and even from television. Lieutenant Mulcahaney was highly respected by all. By Ida Gantry's own observation, she was a good mother.

"No problem, Lieutenant."

"I would consider it a really big favor."

"Glad to help."

About to plunge ahead with more justifications, Norah stopped. "You'll do it?"

"Yes."

"That's wonderful."

"My niece, Alma, that I told you about? She's dating a young man, but she'll be free that night and can help me out."

Norah frowned. The connection escaped her, but now was not the time to try to sort it out. "I appreciate this more than I can say. I'll pay you for the extra hours, of course."

"Thank you. I won't say that's not welcome."

"And I'll be back as soon as I can."

▼ Once again Norah was in the Big Building, this time on her way up to the fifth floor and the latent prints department. She had called her friend Ed Pasquale, and asked to see him. When she presented herself at the reception desk, a pass had been issued. Simple as that. Except that it wasn't simple. Her intent was to enter an office in *police headquarters* illegally! What in God's name had got into her? She should turn right around and walk out.

But she didn't. She got off the elevator at the fifth floor and walked down the corridor to Sergeant Pasquale's door.

The mood of Ed Pasquale and the other detectives in the unit was ebullient over one of the greatest successes in its forty-year history. Norah felt uneasy because she didn't intend to tell Ed the real reason for her visit, but she rationalized that the less he knew, the less trouble he would be in if things went really sour.

She had lifted a number of prints from a crime scene, she told Pasquale. They were smudged, overlapped, but she'd managed to isolate one. Even that was in very poor condition. She placed it humbly before him. Could he, somehow, restore it enough to make it identifiable?

After a brief but intense examination, Pasquale gave Norah a quizzical look. "There's not much here. Can you give me any more information?"

"I took it from the nightstand in Chief Felix's bedroom. I was there with Mrs. Felix's permission," she added. "They were both attacked by an intruder, and as you know, the chief is still in a coma. I was hoping maybe we could trace him through this print."

"Can you give me any idea of how many people touched that nightstand legitimately? Family members, domestics, visitors?"

These were called elimination prints, and if identified could make the job of the expert much easier.

Norah shook her head. "I'm sorry."

Eduardo Pasquale was a handsome man—six foot two, dark-haired, with the famed Roman nose that made him look, in profile, as if he belonged on a classic coin. He had wanted a large family, but had only one child—Cassandra, called Cassie.

Cassie was fifteen when she was seduced by her history teacher, Mr. Black. She wasn't his only conquest, but she was the most recent. A striking girl, raven-haired, much resembling her father, she was the one the neighbors identified as leaving the teacher's apartment on the night he was stabbed to death. She swore she hadn't been there, but refused to say where she had been. Finally, under Norah's gentle but persistent probing, Cassie owned up to having been with a wild bunch drinking and drag racing through the quiet streets of the community—all of it at a distance of thirteen miles from the scene of the murder.

Pasquale bowed his head. "I'll do my best."

It was a matter of making the print identifiable enough to be sent to the State Automated Fingerprint Identification System, known as SAFIS. There it would be put into the computer that stored 3.2 million prints of people who had been arrested. The match could be made in hours, days, or months. Or never. Norah didn't expect the print she had brought to get that far.

"Don't let it make you crazy," she told Pasquale.

He looked at her hard. "You don't need it to make the case?"

On that she had to be honest. "There is no case—so far."

It was still daylight when Norah left her friend's office. However, she didn't leave the building; that would have meant turning in her pass. She spent some time in the women's room listening as the various offices shut down. At 5:45, she went up to the executive floor. It appeared deserted. One glance showed her that Felix's office was closed. At that moment, the lights in Deland's office went out. She ducked around the corner as Ruth Lasker emerged and headed for the elevator at the other end of the corridor.

After the secretary was gone, Norah waited another ten minutes to be sure no one was coming back for any reason. When she was sure the coast was clear, she produced Felix's keys, unlocked his door, and stepped quickly into his anteroom. She felt as though she had carried a sack of stones up a steep hill—and the job hadn't even begun.

The row of filing cabinets behind the secretary's desk was intimidating. Being restricted to the narrow beam of her penlight for illumination didn't make it any easier. There was a song . . . how did it go? Eliminate the negative, accentuate the positive? What was the positive here? What did she hope to find? A name that would link all the Blue Deaths. Unfortunately, that name was not likely to be at the head of any file, but buried somewhere inside. It could appear anywhere in the case record, so that she had to skim long sections before she was able to eliminate and move on.

It took time; it was tedious. The building had barely settled into its night mode and Norah was immersed in the search when the ring of the telephone in the inner office made her jump. It had a lonely sound, much like the sound of a train whistle in the night. It might foretell disaster, the answer to a prayer, or just a wrong number. It rang seven times before the caller gave up.

Norah was shaken. She decided she was wasting time in the outer office. Jim Felix was not likely to have left anything of real importance where anyone who knew how to use a plastic card to slip a lock could get in. Her instinct was to leave, but having come this far, she should at least go through his desk.

The place didn't feel the same without Jim there, Norah thought as she sat at his desk. What would he think if he were to see her there? She hoped she wouldn't find anything, so that he would never have to know. With that she unlocked the center drawer.

It was just about empty. Aside from some personal correspondence referring mostly to social affairs, an envelope which contained pictures of the Chief and Sally taken on their most recent vacation, a couple of scratch pads, some paper clips and rubber bands, there was only one item. It was a book, a slim volume titled *Voodoo: Its Rites and Practices*. She flipped the pages. Several were dog-eared, most of them in the chapter headed "The Conjure: Plants with the Properties to Induce Hypnosis."

There were drawings of these plants—their leaves and berries. She didn't take the time to study them, not then, not there. At this point she didn't dare guess what possession of this book implied. She stuffed it into her ever present pouch, looked around to make sure she hadn't left any sign of her presence, and was about to step out into the corridor when she saw the indicator light over the elevator flashing. Quickly, she retreated. She heard the beep that indicated the elevator had stopped on that floor. The next sound she heard was footsteps coming in her direction. She scurried into the inner office and crouched behind Jim Felix's desk.

The footsteps drew near.

She doused the penlight and waited for them to pass.

But they didn't. They stopped at the outer door. There was a light knock, almost stealthy. "Norah?"

She didn't answer.

"Norah, it's me, Ed. Let me in."

She held her breath.

The door shook. "They know you're in the building. They're looking for you."

She got up, walked around the desk and through the reception area to unlock the outer door. "How do they know I'm in the building?"

"You didn't turn in your pass."

Norah sighed. She hadn't expected Security would be checking so soon, if at all.

"They called me and asked when you had left. I said you were still with me and we were working. They *requested*"—he stressed the word—"that I advise them when you were ready to leave."

Norah groaned. "I'm sorry. I'm sorry if I caused you embarrassment. How did you know where to find me?"

"Come on, Norah! Everybody knows how you feel about Chief

Felix. Everybody knows you're trying to find out what happened to him and to clear his name."

"His name doesn't need clearing. Chief Felix's reputation is impeccable."

"There are all kinds of rumors, Norah. You're out of touch working at home and all."

She flushed. So it was common knowledge! *Never underestimate NYPD's grapevine.*

Pasquale read the dismay on her face. "You should have called and told me what you were up to. I would have been glad to help."

"I didn't want to get you into trouble in case anything went wrong."

"Don't you trust me?"

"It's not a question of trust."

"What then? The print you brought me—no way anybody is ever going to make heads or tails of it. You surely knew that. You surely didn't expect me to waste time on it. So why did you bring it in? It had to be a ruse of some kind."

"No, honestly, it wasn't. Well, not totally. I had hope, not much but some, that you could do something with it. If you did, it could turn out to be crucial. I wasn't trying to fool you."

"I want to be of service to you, Norah. Don't deprive me of the opportunity."

"You don't owe me anything. What I did for Cassie is no more than I would have done for any child."

"You did it for my Cassie and that's what counts with me." Pasquale put a firm period to the discussion. "So, are you through here?"

Norah adjusted the strap of the pouch so that it wouldn't slip off her shoulder. "All through."

"Then I suggest we go back down to my office. Security might just get it into their heads to look in. We'll take the back stairs. They may be monitoring the elevator."

"You used the elevator," she reminded him.

"I couldn't face nine flights going up," he admitted. "It'll be easier going down."

It wasn't. By the time they reached the fifth floor, both were breathing heavily and trying to hide it from the other. Norah made a silent vow to join an exercise class. Pasquale, who liked to box, promised himself more time at the gym.

His hand on the telephone, Ed Pasquale held off. "You're sure there's nothing you want to tell me? Nothing I can do for you?"

"You've already done enough."

"Very well." He lifted the receiver. "This is Sergeant Pasquale in Latent. Lieutenant Mulcahaney is just leaving. We'll be down in a few minutes."

Static garbled the reply, which wasn't anything more than a polite acknowledgment.

"You don't need to escort me. Honestly, it's not necessary."

"Don't be so prickly, Lieutenant. Let me do you this small favor. Also, I want it on the record and witnessed that you left and when you left."

"I suppose that's a good idea."

This time they took the elevator. Together they emerged into the lobby—which, empty, seemed cavernous—and walked side by side, to the security man who stood at the door. He was small and wore a tunic that was too large for him, so that his head seemed to disappear between his shoulder pads. He reminded Norah of a turtle.

"You gave us a scare, Lieutenant," he grumbled as he went through the pages of the register to find her entry. Then he turned the book around and handed her a pen. "We were afraid something had happened to you. You should tell us when you expect to stay late. You too, Sergeant—if you expect a visitor to stay after hours, you should inform us."

The turtle could snap, Norah thought. "We didn't expect the job to take so long." She returned the pen.

"Have you got wheels, or can I give you a lift?" Pasquale asked.

"I'll take the subway."

"I'll walk you to the station."

"Not necessary. I've taken enough of your time. I'm a big girl. I'll be all right."

"Well, if you're sure . . ."

"I'm sure." She smiled at Pasquale, then at the guard. "I'm sorry for the trouble. Goodnight."

She was glad to get out. For one terrible moment, she'd been afraid the turtle wouldn't let her pass. Ridiculous. Then she was afraid he'd ask what she had in her bag. But he didn't. There was no reason in the world that he would suspect she was taking anything out of the building. Stealing, wasn't it? Had the book been found, she could have simply said it was hers. How could anyone prove otherwise? Unfortunately, none of that made her feel any better.

Stopping at the far end of Police Plaza, Norah took several deep, restoring breaths of the soft night air. Everything looked different at night, she thought as she strolled toward the subway station. The streets were dark and deserted; there was almost no traffic, no other pedestrians. She was completely alone. The shadows, soothing at first, turned menacing. She quickened her pace. By the time she reached the station, she was almost running. A busy stop during business hours and when the courts were in session, it was apparently little used in the off hours, but to Norah, at that moment, it was a haven. She flashed her shield case to the token clerk and was buzzed through the turnstile. She took the escalator down to the platform to mix with the handful of passengers waiting for a train.

▼ Norah's intuition had not failed her; a man had been waiting for her outside police headquarters for several hours. Melding into one shadow after another, he had followed her all the way to the subway. He enjoyed the challenge of being close without her knowing. He decided he would get on the train with her and sit . . . well, not beside her, but in the same car.

A train was just then pulling in. Norah, who was far ahead on the platform, had plenty of time to get on. The man was holding back and had to sprint. He got on just as the doors were closing.

▼ There were plenty of empty seats. Norah chose one near a door. As soon as she was settled, she opened her handbag and took out the book she'd found at the back of Jim Felix's drawer. Even the title, *Voodoo: Its Rites and Practices,* was a revelation. She'd always thought of voodoo as a cult with no particular structure, consisting of rituals and spells, never imagining there was enough substance to warrant a book. Were the chantings, the self-hypnosis, the blood sacrifices offerings to a heathen symbol or to a god?

She couldn't concentrate. She felt uneasy, the kind of instinct she had when something bad was about to happen, and which she'd already experienced once that night. She put the book away and began to watch the other riders, but surreptitiously. They were your usual mixed lot: African-Americans, Hispanics, Asians, Caucasians—she'd nearly left them out. Some were sleeping, others reading newspapers, local and foreign. Most stared vacantly ahead, careful not to make eye contact with anyone. A couple of young Chinese women talked in high, piercing voices, like birds that could be heard over the roar and rumble of the train. A man sitting opposite her—very thin, with a coffee-colored complexion and dreadlocks—winked. She immediately turned away and at the same time pulled open the zipper of her bag so that she could get to her gun if need be. When she stole another look, the man with the dreadlocks was ogling the Chinese women.

She must have imagined it. Nevertheless, Norah was relieved when they reached Sixty-eighth Street and Hunter College. That was her stop and she got off.

The man with the dreadlocks did not.

_____

▼ When Norah let herself into her apartment, it was quiet and the lights in the foyer and the front room were turned low. There was a sense of security here, of love, that seemed to wrap itself around her. She moved to the inner hallway and called softly, "Mrs. Gantry? I'm home."

The nanny came out of Patrick's room. "He's just fallen asleep. He tried so hard to stay awake. He kept asking when you'd be back. He said he never went to sleep till you were home. Finally, we made a deal—he'd put on his jammies and get into bed, and I would read to him till you were back." Ida Gantry's smile was full of tenderness. "He fell asleep while I was reading."

"I'm so grateful to you, Mrs. Gantry."

"Glad to help. Why don't you go in and give him a kiss?"

"I don't want to wake him."

"He's a baby. He'll fall asleep again right away."

"All right." Beaming, Norah went to the boy's room. She bent over the sleeping child and kissed him lightly, first on the forehead and then on the lips.

He opened his eyes and looked into hers. "Mama, mama," he said, and closed them again.

How such a moment made a difference in a difficult day, Norah thought. She returned to the kitchen, where Mrs. Gantry was busy at the stove.

"Everything go all right? Tonight, I mean?"

She was curious of course; it was reasonable. "About as expected." Norah couldn't tell her more.

"You look tired. Have you had anything to eat?"

"I'm not hungry."

"Sure you are; you just don't know it. My cousins from Delaware visited last weekend and I cooked up a ham. With the bone I made pea soup. I brought some over. It's delicious, if I do say so myself."

"You're very good to us, Mrs. Gantry."

"It's my pleasure, Lieutenant. Anytime." She waited for Norah to make a specific request.

"That's good to know. Thank you."

It was obvious to Mrs. Gantry that Norah's mind was somewhere else. "I'll be going then."

"All right."

Norah took out Felix's book and began reading those sections he had underscored.

The victim of a conjure has been observed to gradually lose his normal, healthy color, to weaken in strength. He develops flulike symptoms alternating between chills and raging fever. He loses weight and can't hold food in his stomach. He has fits, suffers hallucinations, imagines himself being hunted, and flees, plunging into the jungle of his mind as well as the torments of his body.

"Lieutenant?" Mrs. Gantry cleared her throat. "I'll see you tomorrow."

Norah looked up to see the nanny standing before her in a bright red rain poncho and high rubber boots, a rain bonnet over her flaming red hair and an oversized striped umbrella over her arm.

"It's not raining, Mrs. Gantry."

"They're predicting more to come."

Norah nodded. "I'll see you in the morning then, usual time."

"Of course."

"I'm very grateful for your cooperation tonight. Thank you again."

Mrs. Gantry hesitated. "Get some rest, Lieutenant."

"I will." Before the nanny was out the door, before the click of the lock, Norah was deep in the book again.

No respected conjurer admits to the existence of death conjures, much less to the knowledge of how to inflict one. It is possible to find an unscrupulous practitioner who would undertake to cast such a spell of course, but it is expensive and dangerous because the spell could be reversed and turned against the instigator.

If you could believe that, you could believe anything, Norah thought.

Jim Felix's symptoms matched those described. Obviously, he

knew that, but what made him think they were the result of a con-jure? He must have known that Bill Ciccerone had the same symp-toms and Schiff and Douglas as well, though to a lesser degree. Why had he kept quiet?

Norah thought she knew the answer. It was simple, the only as-pect of this convoluted case so far that was. If James Felix, a three-star chief in the NYPD, should even hint he might be the object of a voodoo curse, he would be laughed out of the department. But no one who saw Chief Felix lying in the hospital on a respirator, with an array of plastic tubes sprouting from his body, would think it was funny. Norah was sure she would remember if Felix had ever been involved in anything to do with voodoo. It must have been before her time.

Maybe one of her old boys would remember.

CHAPTER 15

▼ Norah called Bob Renquist right away. She had a new angle on the case that she wanted to discuss with him and his friends, she told the retired cop. Could he contact them and ask them to come over a little earlier than planned—say, eight o'clock tomorrow morning?

"Sure." Renquist was excited. "Can you give me an idea what this is about?"

"I think it should wait till we're all together."

"Whatever you say, Lieutenant."

"Did Amos and Greg find anything of interest in Bill Ciccerone's files?"

Renquist groaned. "Files is a misnomer, Lieutenant. According to the guys, that basement is like a dump site. There are stacks of papers yellow and brittle with age, water-damaged, in no discernible order. It's a matter of scanning every line to make sure we're not missing anything. They can't even estimate how long it might take to make sense out of it."

Norah thought of her frantic search through Jim Felix's papers. She had been lucky. "We'll compare notes tomorrow," she said.

Though it was still early when she finished with Renquist, Norah was tired. Her mind was crammed with information, allegations, half-formed theories. The most useful thing to do was to get some sleep so she would be fresh in the morning. Once more she looked in on Patrick and made sure the monitor was functioning, then went to her own room and to bed. She fell asleep right away. It was just ten P.M.

She woke at twelve with nausea and an urgent need to get to the bathroom. Only a brief hour later, she was wakened again and had to race to the toilet. Diarrhea troubled her through the night.

At seven, Norah gave up trying to sleep. She had been in bed for nine hours, but her body had had little rest and demanded more. Her eyes were gritty and a gummy discharge made the lids stick together. Her limbs were heavy. She got herself out of bed and staggered to the washbasin. This time she threw up. When she stopped retching, she looked up into the mirror. The face she saw was white and drawn, eyes lackluster, hair limp. But she felt better. She found the thermometer, placed it under her tongue, and sat on the toilet to wait for it to register.

Her temperature was normal; well, maybe a hair over but not significant. She admitted to herself that she had been worried, but it was indigestion after all. She hadn't eaten much these past days—a couple of franks and those on the run. Eating too little and too fast and under stress was as bad as eating too much. She was okay, Norah told herself, and by the time she was dressed and had dressed Patrick and given him his breakfast, she did feel better. Then the phone rang.

Oh no! Not Mrs. Gantry calling to say she couldn't make it, Norah thought with a sinking sensation. *Please God, not that.* "Hello?"

"He's awake!"

Norah recognized the voice right away—Sally Felix.

"He woke up . . . maybe twenty minutes ago. Oh, Norah, I walked into the room and there he was, eyes wide open and looking straight at me. 'Good morning,' he said. He said good morning as though it was any ordinary day." Sally Felix began to cry.

"How wonderful!" Norah's own tears welled up and spilled over. "How's he feeling?"

"Hungry. Isn't that wonderful? He's hungry! He wants a regular, solid breakfast—eggs with bacon, toast, and coffee, but the nurse won't give it to him till the doctor says it's okay." Sally punctuated her words with soft gulps. "I'm so happy."

"When can he go home?"

"The nurse thinks it will be a while before they wean him off the respirator and the various IVs. To take him off too abruptly might be a shock to his system. His own doctor is coming in for a consultation."

"May I come over?" Norah asked. "I'll only stay a few minutes, but I would like to see him." She could hardly wait to hear his story from his own lips.

Sally broke into her thoughts. "Jim says you're welcome at any time. That goes for me too."

"Is there anything I can bring? Anything you or Jim need?"

"There's nothing in this world that I don't already have."

Silently, Norah echoed that.

Next, she called Renquist. While she waited for him to answer his phone, Mrs. Gantry walked in waving a cheery greeting. Then Renquist picked up.

"Good news, Bob. Chief Felix has come out of the coma. He's fully awake . . . Yes, it *is* like a miracle. According to Sally, he shows no signs of ill effects, thank God. I'm on my way over to the hospital. I don't expect to stay long, but it would be helpful if we could move our meeting back, say to eleven?"

"At your convenience, Lieutenant."

Norah was excited by Felix's recovery. He was a good man, one they could ill afford to lose. She was happy for Sally first of all, and for herself she was relieved and eager to hear what he had to say. His evidence might be all that was necessary to prove her theory about the Blue Deaths. At the very least it would confirm she was headed in the right direction.

Suddenly, Norah decided that the navy pants suit she had put on was too somber for the occasion. She went back to the bedroom and changed to a lime-green slip dress with matching jacket. A flick of the hairbrush to give a little bounce to her dark hair, a slash of lipstick, and she was ready. Norah was not one to waste time fussing over her appearance, but as she collected the indispensable pouch and checked her weapon, she took a quick look at herself in the mirror over the bureau. Certainly she looked better than she had earlier. The lime-green was becoming, a good color for her, she thought, and she leaned forward to make a closer inspection.

Norah was not vain, but no one welcomes the appearance of those first lines. The new cream she was trying made her face tingle. In a matter of minutes it took on a slight and becoming flush. According to the directions, you were supposed to apply it generously morning and night for ten days. She was only on the third day and already there was improvement—the frown line between her eyes and the lines above her upper lip had just about disappeared.

▼ It seemed to Norah as she entered the Tower Suites of New York General that there was an unusual amount of activity in the celebrity wing. Nurses, resident doctors, technicians, even porters, appeared energized. The source was Suite C. A constant stream of staff found a reason to pass the half-open door and look in. It was almost as though a patient recovery was a novelty the staff didn't quite know how to deal with.

Norah tapped lightly and then went in.

Jim Felix was in a wheelchair directly facing the door, so that Norah came face-to-face with him immediately. She pulled up short at the change. True, she had been visiting every day, but he had been comatose and she had come expecting to see a sick man. Today she had come looking for the man he used to be. He had lost a lot of weight and that alone would make him look old and frail, she reasoned. *Jim Felix, old and frail!* It was the first time Norah had associated her friend with age and its consequences. His snow-white hair—his pride—was limp and yellowed. The hand that held the fork and played with the food on the tray in front of him was like a claw. At least he'd had his way about the food, Norah thought: he was asserting himself. And he was off the respirator; that was a big step forward.

Before Norah could think of what to say, Felix held out his arms and she bent into his embrace.

"Norah! Thanks for everything you've been doing for me and Sally."

Even his voice was a croaking travesty of what she remembered. "It was nothing."

"There we have a difference of opinion, but we do on a variety of subjects."

"I'm afraid so."

"Don't be. It's always led us to a good result, hasn't it?"

"Yes, it has." Thinking him a bit querulous, which he had every right to be, Norah changed the subject. "How are you feeling?"

"Rested."

The women smiled at each other. The strain eased.

"Can you tell us what happened?" Norah asked. "Unless it's too painful right now. Maybe we should wait?" she asked Sally.

"It's up to Jim. How do you feel about it, sweetheart?"

He looked down at the remains of the scrambled eggs on his plate with distaste. "I thought I was hungry." He pushed them aside, then sighed and looked at Norah. "What do you want to know?"

"We think, from the way you were lying on the bed with the gun in your hand . . ."

"Just a minute. You say I had a gun in my hand? What gun?"

"Yours. Sally says you keep it in the drawer of your nightstand. You were found spread-eagled on the bed with your gun in your hand."

Felix shook his head slowly, helplessly—bewildered, confused, nothing like the capable, self-confident man she knew. Her heart went out to him and Sally. "Maybe we shouldn't chase after this right now. You need a chance to collect yourself."

"I don't remember. It's all a blank."

Norah could see him straining to remember, and feel the fear that overcame him when he couldn't. "You do remember the first part of the evening with Sally?"

"Yes."

"You weren't feeling well, so you decided to stay at home," Norah recapped. "Sally was to attend the dinner without you." Norah paused for his confirmation and also to allow him to take part in the reconstruction.

Felix nodded. "She didn't want to go, but she finally agreed. When she was gone, I fixed myself a scotch on the rocks, then decided I didn't want it and dumped it into the sink. My head was pounding, my stomach heaving. I needed to lie down. I remember thinking I should undress and not having the strength to do it. I may have gotten one shoe off. . . . My God! I've never felt so completely exhausted. I limped to the bed and collapsed. From that moment to the moment I awoke in there"—he pointed—"I don't remember a thing. You have to tell me what happened."

"You thought you had a bad case of the flu," Norah said. "It was when we talked in your office . . ."

"Oh, yes."

"Somewhere along the line you must have begun to suspect it was more than that. When was that?"

"I don't know. I don't recall coming to that conclusion."

"It didn't occur to you that you might somehow be ingesting a drug? Some kind of hypnotic drug?"

Sally gasped and reached for her husband's hand.

"What gives you such an idea?"

"You did some research, read up on the subject." She didn't press hard; Felix was becoming agitated and so was Sally. "You read a book called *Voodoo: Its Rites and Practices.*"

"Voodoo? Come on, Norah." He laughed. "Get real."

To her the laugh sounded hollow. "You even marked certain sections. Your fingerprints will be on the pages." She wondered if Ed Pasquale would help her out on this one.

"This is really too much, Norah." Felix sat up a little straighter. "I know you want to help. Sally has told me how you've been coming here every day and sitting with her." His voice was growing stronger. "We both appreciate that. But voodoo? That's far out even for you."

Norah clenched her jaw and strove to be calm. "There have been cases—"

"You're not going to tell me that someone has a doll with wisps of my hair or nail clippings attached to it and is sticking pins into it?" Felix demanded, his face stern.

Once again, Norah questioned herself. Did she actually believe such a thing? Of course not. How could she? "What I think is that someone introduced drugs into your system."

"How? Just tell me how," he demanded with no trace of leniency.

"I was hoping, I was counting on your being able to tell me."

"There isn't anything I remember," he insisted. "Accept it."

"How about the gun? Why did you take the gun out of the drawer?"

"I don't remember doing that."

Norah persisted doggedly. "Were you taking any over-the-counter medicine for your cold, no matter how innocuous, that was new to you? It might have combined with something in your system to produce an adverse reaction."

Sally broke in. "Leave," she ordered. "Now. Please leave."

There was nothing Norah could do. She should have anticipated that Felix might not remember. It was not unusual in cases like his. As for his dismissing any possibility that his coma might have been drug-induced—well, Sally had been present and maybe he didn't want to worry her, Norah decided. As she found her way out of the hushed silence of the luxe Tower Suites to the noise and bustle of the main lobby, which was more like a railway terminal than a hospital, two questions were uppermost in her mind.

Why had Felix purchased the book on voodoo?

Why had he refused to admit it? In fact, why had he denied any knowledge of it?

▼ She got back home well ahead of the agreed-upon time, but the four ex-cops were there, sitting in the kitchen and having some of Mrs. Gantry's excellent coffee. She was out with Patrick—it being such a gorgeous day and all, they told Norah. So Norah pulled up a chair and while they all had a second cup, she brought them up to speed.

At her mention of voodoo, they gasped and were very still. Sommers and Hardeen looked at the floor. Renquist and Christie exchanged one quick glance which Norah caught but preferred not to interpret.

"There's no doubt that Schiff, Douglas, and Ciccerone had the same symptoms. What we need to know is how the drug got into their systems. And remember this was not a one-shot deal. The drug was fed to these men over an extended period before its cumulative effect made it possible for the perp to deliver the final sentence of death."

"We can't build a case on four guys having the flu!" Christie exclaimed.

"Of course not."

"Well, what then? The gun?"

"Chief Felix has no recollection regarding the gun." She said it with a finality that precluded further discussion.

"So, what do we do?" Christie asked.

"We go through the records and search out every case in which voodoo is even mentioned, going back as far as . . . as far as we need to go."

"That may not be so far," Hardeen announced. Reaching into the side pocket of his wheelchair, he brought out a large manila envelope and very carefully extracted from it a worn newspaper clipping. "We intended to get some background before presenting it to you, but this seems to be the right time. We found it among Bill's papers." He handed it to Norah.

BLACK RADICAL CONVICTED OF MACHINE GUN SLAYINGS EIGHT YEARS AGO: RELEASED, SUES NYPD FOR SIXTEEN MILLION DOLLARS

Norah paused.

"Go on," Hardeen urged. "Read the rest."

Police Commissioner Peter Lundy was outraged to learn yesterday that the city's Office of the Corporation Counsel was prepared to offer a cash settlement to Jean-Marie Leclerc, who had been convicted of the ambush slaying of two cops and two innocent civilians eight years ago.

Leclerc was given a sentence of fifteen years to life. He had already served eight years, filing appeal after appeal, until finally winning, when a judge ruled that the prosecution had willfully withheld evidence that might have cleared him. The police contend that Leclerc machine-gunned two officers on guard at the uptown residence of the then district attorney, who was prosecuting a number of black radicals waging war on the police. Two civilians, a man and his twelve-year-old daughter, were caught in the line of fire. Leclerc was tried three times—the first trial ended in a hung jury, the second in a mistrial, and at the third he was finally convicted. He was dragged from the courtroom screaming revenge.

Norah's mouth was painfully dry, forcing her to pause. Renquist got her a glass of water. She sipped and continued.

Upon release this past December, Leclerc immediately filed a federal suit against the FBI, the NYPD, and the district attorney who had conducted the prosecution against him, charging them with con-

spiracy to wrongfully convict him. Commissioner Lundy vowed not to give in to his demands.

"He's a convicted assassin," Lundy said when interviewed. "He talks about his rights. What about the rights of his victims?"

A photograph accompanied the piece. It showed a soldier in an ill-fitting uniform that gave no clue of nationality. The man who wore it was gaunt. A visored cap was pulled down over his eyes. He had some kind of machine gun tucked under his arm. The photo was of such poor quality that it would be hard to base an identification on it. The setting, a high wall with an iron gate to one side, wasn't much use either.

Norah passed the two items over to Christie and Renquist, who had not seen them.

"Wasn't it early June that Detective Schiff died?" Renquist asked Norah. "And there were two before him. Isn't that right?"

"We'll have to check the exact dates," Norah said. "We need to establish as many links as we can between the Blue Deaths and Leclerc's trials and activities. That means examining the trial transcripts." She turned to Hardeen and Sommers. "You've done such a great job on this. Will you follow it through?"

Next she addressed Renquist and Christie. "Get everything you can on Leclerc—his history, where he comes from, his past and his present. Find out where he's living now, who his friends are, if he has any. You know what we need."

"No problem, Lieutenant. In order to file his various suits, he had to give an address." Sommers was eager, but Hardeen hung back.

"Excuse me, Lieutenant, but assuming this guy is the one we're after, that he might be going around killing off the cops who testified against him in his three trials—how come nobody caught on?"

"Do you remember all the cases you worked eight years ago?" Norah asked.

"I wasn't involved in anything like this. I would have remembered this."

So would she, Norah thought, but she said, "Maybe they did." Then she quoted Jim Felix. "But if one of them had stepped forward and said his cough and fever were caused by a voodoo curse, what reaction do you think he would have got?"

"What do you think, Lieutenant? Could it be a voodoo curse?"

"That's what the perp wants us to believe."

CHAPTER 16

▼ Norah wrestled with the problem at every free moment. As she no longer reported for regular duty, she had plenty of them.

The weather turned hot. Norah's household routine was established. Mrs. Gantry proved reliable and responsible and Patrick became attached to her. If Norah could have found someone like Ida Gantry to cover nights and weekends, she could have gone back to her job. Meantime, the investigation was well in hand. There were two meetings a day with the men she thought of as her "seniors," one in the morning to discuss the day's goals and another at night to review what had been accomplished in between. But for her constant, nagging headaches—sinus headaches, she was prone to them—all was as well as could be expected under the circumstances. The headaches usually cleared by midmorning. At night she experienced a slight sinus drip, but that was nothing. It did occur to her that the symptoms were somewhat like those of the men whose deaths she was investigating, but she shook that idea off. First of all, the symptoms were mild. Second, she was in no way connected to Leclerc. He didn't even know that she existed.

As the days passed, Norah and her seniors amassed an impressive amount of information. The picture they built was of a professional killer.

Jean-Marie Leclerc came from Port-au-Prince, Haiti. Born in poverty and destined to live in poverty, Leclerc did not passively accept his fate. He studied hard, and at the first opportunity he joined the army. He distinguished himself from the rank and file by volunteering for every special duty no matter how onerous, showing no squeamishness, no revulsion, whatever the bloody task. He advanced quickly. The peak of success was his appointment to the President's personal guard, the infamous *tonton macoutes*. This elite group was known and feared by the entire populace. Its members terrorized the people. They stole, raped, and murdered without fear of retaliation. As long as "Papa Doc" Duvalier remained in power, the *tonton macoutes* spread terror and lived high. Upon the elder Duvalier's death, there was a brief period of instability which threatened Leclerc and his like, until Duvalier's son, "Baby Doc," took control and it seemed all would be as before.

But after having had a taste of freedom, the people were not so easily cowed. They rose up and drove Baby Doc out of the country and off the island. Leclerc was one of the personal guards who fled with him and his family into exile. But life in Grenoble—France was the only country that would accept them—was too restricted. Baby Doc could neither pay for nor protect his henchmen's riotous lifestyle. Leclerc moved to New York, where he was attached, unofficially, to the consulate and given assignments consistent with those he'd carried out in his homeland.

Unfortunately for him, he had gone too far in openly gunning down the two cops and the two civilians in front of the DA's house. In high council it was decided not to protect him but to leave him to American justice. He was tried, convicted, and sentenced. He managed to win release after eight years.

Upon release, Leclerc lost no time in bringing his various suits. Not only did he have to give his address, but he was required to hold himself available. So Renquist and Christie had no trouble finding him. They watched him for a couple of days, but didn't learn much. He lived in a single-room occupancy in the Village. He ate his meals in a local bar and grill, but he never drank anything alcoholic. The balance of the day was spent in the public library in the reference room. He had no friends, at least insofar as his neighbors could tell. The super said he paid his rent and his utilities on time and was no trouble to anyone. The two ex-cops took pictures of him as he went in and out. They showed a figure in a long, loose raincoat and a floppy fedora.

Meanwhile, Hardeen and Sommers went through the transcripts and learned the identities of those who appeared against Leclerc in his trials. To no one's surprise, they included Officers Schiff and Ciccerone.

What happened was this: Schiff and Ciccerone had been posted as guards inside the DA's residence. The other two uniforms, Kramer and Foxworth, were posted outside. At the change of shifts, as the men were milling around on the sidewalk in front of the building, a van that had been moving slowly down the block stopped, the back doors opened, and six men wearing black ski masks and carrying submachine guns jumped out. They immediately began shooting indiscriminately. Everybody ran for cover. Two of the cops and two innocent bystanders didn't make it.

Schiff and Ciccerone did—Schiff remained unscathed; Ciccerone took a bullet in the gut but survived to testify against Leclerc. Both stood firm in pointing to him as one of the perpetrators. Still, the trial ended in a hung jury.

▼ "Good work," Norah congratulated her seniors, but she was bemused.

They could see it.

"What's wrong, Lieutenant?" Renquist asked.

"Nothing at all." She should have been elated, but she wasn't. She couldn't explain it to herself, so how could she explain it to them? Besides which, she didn't want to spoil their moment, their sense of achievement. "Did the same witnesses testify at each trial?" She asked the question with no clear purpose in mind.

Sommers blanched. "No. I'm sorry, Lieutenant. We should have, but we thought . . . We had gone through so many documents . . . once we noted the connection . . ." He sighed. "That's all you had asked for."

"Right. It *is* all I had asked for."

"We'll go back . . ."

"No need right now." Norah had a sore throat and she didn't feel well.

"Should we go to the DA with what we've got?"

"No, I have to talk to Captain Jacoby first. He'll probably want to go to Chief Deland."

"Maybe it would be good to consult with Chief Felix. After all, he has a stake in this."

This from Hardeen, who seldom volunteered anything.

"He's not very receptive at the moment." Nor was she, Norah thought. "Why don't we sleep on it and decide what to do when we meet tomorrow." A sharp jab inside her head produced a temporarily blinding flash. She winced.

Christie noticed. "You okay, Lieutenant?"

"Just a headache. It'll pass."

"Get some rest, Lieutenant. See you in the morning."

▼ As soon as they were gone, Norah went to her room to lie down, but she didn't rest. She tried to think, to decide what the next step should be, but the headache got in the way. The room was dark, but when she opened her eyes she saw blobs of colored lights coming at her like a shower of meteorites. If she kept her eyes closed, the room pitched and she felt she was on a raft in stormy seas, and she had to fight off the nausea. What was happening to her?

She woke early the next morning feeling much better. The

headache was just about gone, her throat okay, and her vision normal. Thank God. She dressed and went in to Patrick. At eight on the dot, Mrs. Gantry put her key in the lock and the telephone rang.

"Norah? It's me, Sally. I'm sorry to wake you . . ."

"You haven't wakened me."

"Norah, something terrible has happened. I don't know what to do."

"Slow down. Take a deep breath. . . . That's the way. Once more. Now, tell me what this is all about."

"Jim fell asleep and I can't wake him up."

Dear God! Norah thought. "How do you mean—fell asleep? He fell asleep last night and you can't wake him this morning?"

"No, no. He was fine this morning. He got up; *then* he fell asleep after breakfast."

"And you can't wake him."

"I shook him and slapped him. He doesn't respond. What should I do?"

"For starters, call nine-one-one."

"I've already done that."

"Good. That's good. You should also call his doctor."

"I've done that too. He's on his way over. Oh, Norah, it's even worse than before. Is he going to die?"

"Of course not. Get hold of yourself, Sally."

▼ When Norah arrived at the Felix residence, an EMS unit was already double-parked in front of the building, along with a couple of patrol cars. Inside, the elegant lobby was transformed. Gone was the hush of wealth; the air crackled with energy and the static of cellular phones. The very walls vibrated with the vitality of the youthful paramedics and the police as they passed back and forth.

Norah showed her ID to the uniform at the elevator and was allowed to get on. Getting off at the eighteenth floor, she was challenged again. It wasn't often that the response to an emergency was so swift or that so many turned out, but James Felix was, after all, one of the top men in the department, she thought as she walked down the hall to the Felixes' apartment. There no one challenged her and she went right in.

Police— uniformed and plainclothes, along with technicians and the emergency team—were clustered at the open arch to the living room, their backs to Norah.

"Excuse me," she said, trying to make her way through. "Pardon. Please. Thank you." She stumbled through to the front and came up short at the sight of Chief Felix seated in an armchair, conducting what very much resembled a press conference. Except that none of the press were present. He was still in robe and pajamas. His face was pale but shaven. Sally stood just back of him, her hand on his shoulder.

"I'm all right," he announced. "I don't need to go to the hospital. I don't want to go to the hospital."

"Your blood pressure is good, Chief. Your temperature is a couple of lines over normal, nothing to worry about. Just the same, it would be wise for you to get a complete checkup." The young paramedic looked and sounded tired. Norah wondered how many times during one tour he made this same speech.

"No," Felix replied, in much the same way and for the same reason. "I've had enough tests and checkups to last me the rest of my life. I've had blood drawn, X rays, CAT scans, MRIs, and I don't know what all. None of it has helped or told us anything." Having said that, Felix slumped back, spent. As Sally bent to him quickly, he reached up and patted her hand reassuringly.

Norah stepped forward. "You can't make him go if he doesn't want to."

"No, ma'am, we can't," the paramedic acknowledged, "but we feel strongly that he should go, and if you're his friend, we urge you to tell him the same. And you too, Mrs. Felix."

"I'm awake. I'm alert, I'm coherent," Felix stated; then, with a trace of his normal humor, he added, "At least, I think I am." He was rewarded with a ripple of laughter. "And as I've been reminded today is the Fourth of July, I'm declaring my independence."

More laughter.

"What can they do for me in the hospital? I haven't had much solid food in the past few days and I'm weak, so I had a fainting spell. That's all."

"Our own family doctor is on his way," Sally Felix said.

"Well, in that case . . ." The paramedic shrugged. "We're out of here."

"I appreciate your concern."

"It's okay, Chief. Good luck to you and you too, Mrs. Felix." He nodded to Norah.

The medics left and Felix dismissed the others. Finally, Felix and his wife and Norah were alone.

"Now tell me what happened," Norah said.

Felix frowned. "Nothing happened. I had a fainting spell. Sally panicked, understandably. While she was calling everyone she could think of to help, I came out of it."

"What brought it on?"

"I have no idea."

"You must have."

They were snapping at each other. Was it possible he really had no idea? Norah wanted to believe that. She took another tack. "You know what we're looking for, Jim. Think. Start with when you got up this morning. How did you feel?"

"Fine," he replied promptly. "Better than I had expected."

"What time was it?"

"Well, I woke at five-thirty, but I didn't get up. I lay still so as not to disturb Sally."

"I was awake and lying still so as not to disturb you," Sally said.

"We both got up at six," Felix continued. "Sally went to the kitchen to fix breakfast and I went into the bathroom to shave. She called me when she was ready, and we ate."

"What did you have?"

"Eggs sunny side up, Canadian bacon, toast, and of course, coffee. It was delicious." He beamed on his wife. "Sally was the only one who handled the food, and you can't honestly think . . ."

"Of course not. What happened next?"

"Suddenly I felt queasy; I don't know why. I thought maybe the cold was back."

"You're going to pass this off as the result of a cold?"

"That's right. Sally shouldn't have called you."

"I'm glad she did, because I have symptoms very much like yours, though I haven't fainted. I'm all right in the morning as a rule, but as the day progresses I get this terrible, tired feeling. My legs won't hold me up. I'm hot, then cold. I have pounding headaches."

"It sounds like the flu. There's a lot of it around."

"Particularly in the department."

She dropped it like a time bomb and they both worked around it cautiously.

"How did you happen to be reading up on voodoo?"

"Voodoo?" Jim Felix repeated.

"*Voodoo: Its Rites and Practices.* How did you happen to be reading it just at this time?"

Felix shook his head. "Ah, Norah . . ."

"Why did you think it might be pertinent?"

Felix's green eyes narrowed and sharpened. "Where did you find the book?" he challenged.

She raised her chin and met the challenge. "In your office, in the top drawer of your desk."

"You had no business there."

"I was trying to help."

He groaned. "I'm sure you were."

"Why did you mark the chapter on conjuring?" she asked, almost plaintively. "According to the book, for a conjure to succeed, the victim must first be rendered vulnerable by ingesting certain drugs. It mentions some that can be harvested, plants common in the Haitian countryside, and explains how to prepare them. The author dwells on the difficulty of introducing the drug into the intended victim's bloodstream without his being aware. The object is for the drug to enter the system. It doesn't have to be by mouth. It can be through the skin."

Norah paused, waiting for Jim to say something, to explain, to make it right. When it appeared that he wouldn't, not yet anyway, she went on.

"He tells of one clever solution, which was to dry the berries of the plant, grind them into a fine powder, and scatter it on the door-mat at the victim's front door. In the primitive village where he lived, everyone went barefoot. So the victim would rub his bare feet on the mat before entering his house and the powder would be absorbed through the skin with the perspiration. The effect was cumulative. The symptoms fluctuated in severity. Each time he went in or out, the victim took more of the drug into his system, until finally he became ill and sometimes died.

"But we are not living in a primitive village. We all wear shoes. Sprinkling the powder into food or mixing it into a drink like coffee or wine would seem a more likely method, except that as it has to be ingested over a period of time, someone close to the intended victim has to do it. Do you have a new cook?"

Sally answered. "We don't have a cook anymore. Cooks are fussy about people being on time for meals and Jim's hours are unpredictable. So mostly we order up from a little restaurant on the corner—Chez Pepe."

"How long have you been doing that?"

"Not long, maybe since the start of the year. But we've been eating in the restaurant since we were married. It's close by, cozy, and the food is excellent."

"Is it possible the perp got himself a job at Chez Pepe with the express purpose of tampering with your food?" Norah suggested.

"How would he know which order was mine and which was Sally's?" Felix asked.

A reasonable concern, Norah thought.

"I don't eat meat," Sally pointed out. "They know that at the restaurant."

"Good enough. That would explain how the drug was administered to you, but what about the others? We need to know the agent which served to carry the drug, and it has to be some ordinary thing you all use. Since you all thought you had a cold, it could be a cold medicine. Even eyedrops!"

"No." Felix was emphatic.

"Let's take a look at your medicine cabinet."

Felix sighed. "You don't give up, do you?" He grinned. He got up slowly, using both hands to steady himself, with Norah and Sally on either side ready to assist him if he wavered. But he didn't. He led the way to the master bedroom and his bathroom. Sally had her own.

"See for yourself."

Norah immediately pounced on a can of air freshener and sniffed it cautiously.

"How could that have been contaminated? If it had been, Sally would have been affected too," Felix pointed out.

But Norah had found something else. "What's this?" She pointed to a small bottle of green glass.

"Aftershave balm."

"I know. I mean this." She indicated a label pasted across the front of the bottle which said: *Sample—not for resale.*

"It came in the mail. A promotion, obviously. I tried it and liked it and I've been using it more or less regularly, except when . . . when I was in the hospital."

"While you were there the effects wore off."

Norah could visualize Jim Felix pouring out some of the creamy liquid into a cupped hand and slapping it vigorously over his jowls. He would just have shaved and there would be nicks and scratches to aid the absorption. "Have you resumed using it since you came home?"

"Not till this morning."

"Don't use it anymore."

CHAPTER 17

▼ Norah headed for home full of ideas and plans.

The jar of replenishing cream she had been using lately with what appeared to be beneficial results had come to her through the mail as a promotion. Unfortunately, she had thrown away the container, so she wasn't able to tell where it had come from, but that wasn't as important as the banner across the top of the jar: *Sample—not for resale.* Norah was convinced that the dizzy spells, nausea, and all the other symptoms she had been experiencing were as directly related to her use of the cream as Felix's were to his use of the balm.

It was after eleven when she got back to her apartment, and she found the team waiting in the kitchen. Renquist and Christie were playing chess on a small, portable board; the other two were kibitzing. At her arrival, everything stopped. Sommers jumped to his feet to pull out a chair for her.

"Take a load off, Lieutenant."

"Thanks."

"What's up?"

She told them in some detail.

They were enthusiastic. They applauded.

"Way to go, Lieutenant."

"Nice work."

"You figure Bill and the others got the same stuff through the mail and it accounted for their strange behavior?" Hardeen asked.

"I think it's very likely."

"Poor Bill. We thought he was losing it." Sommers sighed. "Should we go through his stuff once more now that we know what we're looking for?"

"His daughter pretty much cleaned out everything that had any apparent value," Norah told him.

"How about the other two—Schiff and Douglas? I suppose the same applies?"

"Schiff's apartment has already been rented to another tenant and I doubt anybody would save a half-used bottle of aftershave." She paused thoughtfully. "That goes for the Douglas home too, I'm afraid. Try, if you want to. It's all right with me."

"Why don't we get the Chief's aftershave analyzed?" Hardeen looked around at them, his pink and white face glowing.

"Chief Felix is taking care of that himself." He hadn't specifically said so, but Norah was sure he would. "I'm not officially on the case," she reminded them.

They nodded, but clearly they were disappointed.

"You'll see a copy of the report, of course." Hardeen indicated they would make do with that.

"Of course," Norah echoed, but suddenly she wasn't so sure. "I received something similar in the mail recently, a jar of face cream. Since I started using it, I've had symptoms very similar to the Chief's and to those you've described. I thought I was coming down with a cold. Now I'm not so sure."

The men were shocked, their faces grim.

"We've got to get that analyzed. Right away, Lieutenant," Renquist urged. "In the meantime, you've got to be real careful. Watch what you eat and drink and what you inhale. And you shouldn't be alone. One of us should be with you at all times."

"Come on, Greg!" Norah paused. "I appreciate your concern." She laughed, but she was touched. "I don't need a baby-sitter."

"No offense, Lieutenant."

"Of course not." She paused again, took a deep breath, held it, and then slowly released it. "Even if we had all the evidence and the lab confirmed the presence of the drug in each sample, we would still have to prove that it was Leclerc who put it there. Since we can't do that, we have to tempt him into making another try.

"We'll start right away with round-the-clock surveillance. I want to cover him in eight-hour shifts with Sommers the swing man," Norah said. That would make only a skeleton crew. Standard procedure required two men per tour, plus two as backup and two as swing, but nobody complained.

"And we don't really care whether he makes us or not. In fact, let him know he's being watched." She warmed to the plan as she laid it out.

No sooner had the men left for their assignments than Norah realized she had overlooked a major problem—getting Patrick out of the way. Fortunately, Mrs. Gantry agreed to take him to her home for a couple of nights. Norah was relieved but also shaken at having come so close to forgetting about the child. A real mother would have thought of her son first. A real investigator would not be relying on the help of civilians. She was doing a balancing act between the two, and if she wasn't careful, she would fail in both.

"You're going to visit Mrs. Gantry and her niece, sweetheart," Norah explained to Patrick as they were packing his little bag. "You're going to stay over with them for a couple of nights."

"Why?"

For a moment that stumped Norah. "It's a secret. I can't tell you now."

"Are you coming with us?"

"Maybe another time. So now you be a good boy, Patrick, and do what Mrs. Gantry says." Down on one knee, Norah buttoned his jacket, set his cap on his blond head, and hugged him close.

"Don't cry, Mama."

"I'm not crying, darling. I've just got something in my eye."

Mrs. Gantry stepped forward to take him. "Don't worry, Lieutenant, he'll be fine, and if you need him to stay awhile longer, that's okay. I've made the arrangements open-ended."

"Thanks, but I don't think it will be necessary," Norah replied. *Not a day, not an hour, not a minute longer. In fact, never again.*

She saw them out, waiting at the apartment door for a final look as they got into the elevator. With Patrick gone to safety, she could settle down to review the transcripts, and to fine-tune the plan.

▼ Leclerc entered his favorite restaurant on Second Avenue. He knew the place well. A couple of neighborhood youth gangs hung out there, so there was always a police presence, if not at hand, then readily available. He ordered a medium Big Mac, fries, and coffee. He paid for it and carried the tray to a table at the rear that allowed him a good view of everyone who came in or went out.

They weren't bad for retirees, Leclerc admitted grudgingly, but not in his class, as he was about to demonstrate. He waited as the tall, skinny one with all the hair and the beard entered and was followed by the short, square one with rosy cheeks. They went to separate tables. He waited some more as each took his turn at the counter and brought his food back. They had just started to eat, when Leclerc shot to his feet and in so doing knocked his own tray and what was on it to the floor. He turned on Christie, who was nearest.

"You did that on purpose," he shouted. "You've been following

me! Don't think I don't know it. Where are the cops? I want a cop!"
He looked around wildly. "Somebody get the cops!"

Renquist and Christie remained frozen as Leclerc walked out to
the street and disappeared around the corner.

▼ At home, Norah called her good friend Allan Stemhagen at Metro-
Media. She gave him a very big scoop: *Chief James Felix has been
stricken a second time by a mysterious malady, apparently the same
one that felled him a short time ago.*

The breaking story was picked up by radio and television. As the
news spread, so did concern for his recovery. His wife, Sally, refused to send him back to the hospital, so reporters and TV crews
kept watch outside his building through the night. At break of day a
message was sent down: *Chief James Felix has passed away.*

The first feeling was one of dismay at the speed of it. The early
newscasts gave testimony to his life— to his character and his career,
to the prospects that would not now be fulfilled. Mention was made
of Sally Felix, a former Broadway actress who gave up her own career to support his. The one great disappointment of their happy
marriage was not having children.

*All the NYPD mourns. Funeral arrangements to be announced
later.*

Norah turned the set off. She got up and out of the chair she had
sat in all that restless night, and stretched.

With the death of James Felix, she now knew, every police witness who had testified against Leclerc at his three trials was gone. He
should be satisfied. He should pack his bags and go home. As the
killer of five cops—six including Chief Felix—he must know that he
would be hunted for the rest of his life. As long as there was one person alive who could implicate him in their deaths, he would remain
at risk.

She was that one, Norah thought. She posed the threat and she had no doubt he intended to get rid of her as he had the others. There was nothing for her to do but wait. The next move was his.

▼ Evil flourishes in the dark. Night nurtures crime. Norah had been up all of the last night, the night Jim Felix died, and would probably be up again this night and who knew how many after that. So she should get some rest while she could. But nobody in the department was getting much rest; of that she was sure. No matter what her status, she should be with them to share in the mourning. She should stand with the men and women who had known and admired and respected James Augustus Felix. She should be with Sally.

The day at the funeral home was a mosaic of details, filled with small irritations: flowers sent to the wrong funeral home; squabbles over press accreditation for the funeral; allocation of tickets to celebrities, with the constant jockeying for position. Norah had never participated in anything like it and vowed she never would again. It was much worse for Sally, of course.

Late in the afternoon, Norah called Dr. Merlin, the Felixes' physician, and asked him to come and see Sally and give her something to slow her down. At five, Sally caved in and allowed Norah to take her home and hand her over to the housekeeper, with doctor's orders to put her to bed.

Then Norah went home herself. It seemed strange without Patrick there—lonely, empty. She was struck anew at how much a part of her life the boy had become. No—not a part, but the core. So instead of brooding she should concentrate on the things that would make it possible to bring him back. There were approximately three hours of daylight left. Nothing would happen till dark.

Norah woke with a start as night crept over the city. The digital alarm on her nightstand glowed 9:13. There was no time to shower and change, only to go into the bathroom and splash cold water on her face. Catching a look at herself in the mirror over the basin, Norah was startled by the face that looked back at her. She knew she'd lost weight these past few days but she hadn't realized how much. She was almost gaunt. Her skin, which lately had had a becoming flush, due to the drug-laced cream of course, was ashen. Her eyes were larger than ever. Her always dominant jaw quivered. *Stop,* she told herself. She was behaving as though the sting had already failed. She willed her chin to stay steady.

At nine-thirty, the seniors arrived. They were tense too, their normal badinage much restricted. The plan had been discussed that morning. It was evident that the seniors still had reservations.

"Why doesn't he hop a plane and get out while he still can?" Hardeen grumbled.

"Because it's not in his nature to run," Norah answered. "He's always been the hunter, never the hunted. I'm a loose cannon to him. He needs to get rid of me. We're giving him the opportunity to do it at a time and place of our choosing."

She could see they weren't totally convinced. Norah's stomach dropped. She couldn't go into this without full support. Halfhearted wasn't good enough.

"I don't want this hanging over me for the rest of my life!" she exclaimed. "I want it over so I can bring my son home again. I want to get my job back."

She continued. "The man is an assassin, a hired killer. We don't know how many he's killed in his own country. Here, he's killed a man as dear to me as a father. For that alone I have to make at least one final attempt to get him. You don't have the stake in this that I do. I realize that, and if you don't want to take part, I understand. You can bow out with no hard feelings."

There was a moment of embarrassed silence. Renquist cleared his throat.

"Who said anything about quitting?"

There remained only to go over the assignments.

Renquist and Christie would stay upstairs with Norah. Hardeen in his wheelchair would be down in the lobby as lookout to alert Norah and the others when the perp was on his way up.

Hopes shifted from flat dejection to high determination. Nevertheless, nobody believed it would be over quickly, so Sommers was sent home to rest to resume surveillance the next day—if it should prove necessary.

It was a night for disappointment and frustration. Norah's nerves were on edge. The headache and other maladies she'd been plagued with returned. She hadn't touched the jar of face cream, but she knew that it was characteristic of certain drugs that their effects could recur spontaneously days, weeks, or even months after their use had been discontinued. She hadn't confided this to her new friends.

At four A.M., Norah called it a night and sent everyone home.

Nothing happened that day, and the next night was similar to the first. Everyone was feeling the strain. Nobody wanted to admit it. Nobody mentioned giving up.

The third night was as uneventful as the first two. Norah missed Patrick. She talked to him at least twice a day by telephone, but it wasn't enough for either of them. For all Mrs. Gantry's kindness, Patrick kept asking when he could come home.

On the fourth night of frustration, Norah faced reality.

"He knows we've set a trap," she announced to the weary, discouraged troops. "We can wait till Doomsday, but he's not going to show. He knows I'm not alone."

"What should we do?" Renquist as usual spoke for the group.

"Go home."

"And leave you without backup? No way."

Brave words, Norah thought, but they couldn't support them; they were too old. She shook her head sadly. "Go home."

"No, we can't leave you alone," Christie said. "Maybe we can make it look like you're alone. We can walk out the front . . ."

"The man isn't stupid, Tom. You've found that out firsthand. No, when you leave, you have to really leave."

"Compromise, Lieutenant," Renquist broke in. "We leave the building and head for the subway. As we go down, we separate and take different stairs. This poses a dilemma. Which one should he follow?"

"Why should he follow either one? It's me he's interested in. No. I'm calling it off."

There was a moment of silence.

"Maybe that's best," Bob Renquist said.

▼ To make it look like suicide, Leclerc needed the victim's gun. Norah had no intention of giving him the slightest chance of putting his hands on it, so she locked it in her safe deposit box at the bank. So she was without backup and without a weapon.

There was, of course, one way of convincing the perp that she had indeed given up trying to trap him, Norah thought, and that was to bring Patrick home. He would surely know all about her and the boy, their history. He must have seen them together many times and he would be able to recognize Patrick. He would know also that she would never bring her son home if there was any possibility of violence or danger. And he would be right.

Common sense argued that Patrick and Mrs. Gantry would never have to come anywhere near Jean-Marie Leclerc. They would never even be in the same room. In fact, they would be gone before Leclerc got upstairs.

She could call Mrs. Gantry now—it wasn't that late—and tell her to pack Patrick's suitcase and call a taxi. They could enter the building through the front, take the front elevator to the second floor and change to the service elevator, ride down again to the ground floor. They would then go out the back and return to Mrs. Gantry's place. It was simple and safe. What effect would it have on the child? If they told him it was a game, would he believe it? Having been wakened in the night, dressed hurriedly, shuttled back and forth, he would be frightened, traumatized. How could she ever explain it to him? No use to dwell on it, she thought. If she was going to do it, she had to do it fast. Tonight. Now. She went to her desk and picked up the phone and dialed Mrs. Gantry's number. She waited for it to ring and then hung up before the nanny could possibly answer.

She couldn't do it. She couldn't *use* Patrick. Norah shuddered at how close she'd come to doing just that.

What other way was there to lure Leclerc into the confrontation? She swiveled her chair around so she could look out the window at the quiet street below. Was he even out there? Norah wondered as she began to turn off the lights one by one. Was she playing out the charade to an empty house? she asked herself, and went to her bedroom and there switched off the last light in the apartment. Though she had just about convinced herself that it was all futile, she stood silent and motionless in the dark, watching and listening for the slightest sign of activity. She pulled up a chair—maybe from this angle she would have a better view. She sat down to wait. Gradually, the tension eased. She was nodding when she heard the click of the lock on her front door. She held her breath. He was here.

As quietly as she could, Norah made her way to the bedroom door. Having turned her back to the street and the light from the streetlamps, she had trouble seeing. She misjudged the width of the bed and gouged her calf on the corner of the frame. She could feel the blood running down her leg, but ignored it. With small, cautious steps, she moved toward the door between bedroom and living room. After a short while, as her eyes became accustomed to the dark, she managed to make out a mass that was moving—in her direction.

Her heart was pounding; there was a roaring in her ears. This was the moment she'd been working toward, but in order to achieve it, she'd been forced to get rid of the backup. So he had the first round.

Joe had always emphasized that the detective's greatest weapon was interrogation. At the same time, he'd warned, *Watch your rear.* He would not have been pleased with this situation. No more was she. Through the years and many cases, Norah Mulcahaney had faced many kinds of killers, but never before an executioner.

"I was beginning to think you wouldn't come," she charged, initiating the attack despite the fact that she could only direct her words in the general direction of the mass, which had now stopped moving.

"Like you, I was waiting for the propitious moment."

The intruder spoke with the soft vowels and typical lilt of Haiti. "You are a smart lady, but I am smarter. Your preparations were obvious—sending your son away, for instance. That told me all I needed to know. And the old men you assigned to following me . . . an insult, Lieutenant. They were so clumsy."

Clumsy enough to get you up here, Norah thought. But now that he was here, she didn't know what to do with him. If she managed somehow to get him to admit his guilt, there was no one to witness it. She had not prepared well for this.

"Shall we sit down?" Without waiting for an answer, she backed up and sat on the edge of the bed. "And light. We need light." She reached under the shade of the bedside lamp for the switch.

"No! No light. This is good enough for now."

He didn't want her to get a good look at him. So he wasn't necessarily committed to killing her. Norah squinted in the light from the street. She could make out the outlines of a tall, thin man. A loose, wrinkled raincoat camouflaged just how thin he was, and a battered fedora hid his face. Nevertheless, from beneath its wide brim his eyes gleamed like the yellow eyes of a cat. "We're wasting time," he sighed, and suddenly, out of nowhere, there was a gun in his hand.

Norah jumped up. He'd been so quick she hadn't seen him draw. She raised her arms. "I'm not carrying."

"Where's your piece? Get it."

"I don't have it. I don't keep it in the house."

"That's a lie," he snarled. "Get it. Now! Or else."

"Or else what?" Having survived this far, Norah felt some of her courage returning. "Or else you'll kill me? You'll kill me anyway, but you want to do it with my gun so it will look like suicide, same as the others." She paused, took a deep breath, squared her shoulders, and raised her chin. "I'm not going to help you. You'll have to use your own piece and take your chances with a murder charge."

"I'll kill your son."

He said it without a trace of emotion. Norah shuddered at the coldness and then matched it. "He's in a safe place where you can't touch him."

"You can't keep him hidden forever."

"I have friends who will protect him. You can kill me, but you won't get away with it, I promise you. My friends know who you are. If you're thinking about fleeing to your own country, I advise against it. The authorities have been alerted and will pick you up and turn you over to us." Which wasn't true, but would be if she got out of that room alive. *God help me and put the right words in my mouth.* "On the other hand, they may decide to prosecute you themselves; they have good cause." As she talked, Norah edged toward the telephone.

He laughed, and she marveled that he was able to.

"It's a big world and I have big money supplied to me by your own FBI. Interesting how your system works, isn't it? First, you put me through a duplicitous trial and convict me. Then you release me and pay me for my pain and suffering. Did you know that I'm in line for additional funds from the Department of Correction and from your NYPD? But I can't wait around for it. And that's because of your meddling, Lieutenant."

Lips twisted in a sneer, Leclerc raised the Colt .45, which at that range was guaranteed to blow her away. Norah held her breath. In the heavy silence the click as the safety was released was ominously loud.

"Drop it!"

The lights came on everywhere.

Jim Felix appeared just outside the doorway, gun pointed at Leclerc.

Norah threw herself across the bed and rolled over and down to the floor on the other side.

Leclerc stared at Jim Felix in horror. "You!" he gasped. "You," he repeated. "I thought . . . you were supposed to be . . . They said you were dead."

"Sorry to disappoint you," Felix replied. "Drop the gun. Now!"

As Leclerc hesitated, Felix fired, hitting the hand in which he held the gun. Blood spurted from the wound. Leclerc looked at it in surprise. He held his hand out to Norah as though to show her the injury, and Felix fired again—two shots in quick succession, one to the shoulder, the other directly into his face.

Leclerc remained standing, still holding his gun, bewildered.

"No!" Crouched behind the bed, Norah cried out to Felix. "No! Stop!"

Felix didn't appear to hear her. He fired once more. At last, the onetime *tonton macoute,* covered in blood, sank slowly to his knees.

Going to the fallen man, Norah felt at the side of his jaw for the carotid pulse, the pulse of life. After a few moments, she looked up at Jim Felix.

"He's gone."

"He was going to shoot you," Felix said in a flat voice.

"You didn't have to kill him."

"I thought he was going to kill you."

CHAPTER 18

▼ The usual crime scene personnel answered the call. As soon as they discovered who was involved—Chief James Felix, the C of D's right-hand man (wasn't he supposed to be dead?), and Lieutenant Norah Mulcahaney (wasn't she supposed to be on suspension?)—a heavy restraint fell upon them. They walked on tiptoe and spoke in hushed tones. Norah had called the complaint in directly to the squad at the Two-Oh. Ferdi Arenas had answered. Chief Felix had himself made the call to his boss, Chief Deland, who had gotten out of bed and come over. Upon his arrival, the atmosphere in Norah's bedroom became even more tense.

Having made a quick and experienced survey of the situation, Deland drew his CEO to one side. "You okay, Jim?"

Felix nodded.

"Lieutenant?"

"I'm fine, sir, thank you."

Back to Felix. "What happened?"

"He had his gun on her, I had to move fast. I had no choice. I had to shoot first—he had already killed five good men. I couldn't risk . . ."

"Of course not," Deland agreed. And to Norah once more: "Lieutenant?"

She nodded. "He would have shot us both."

The Chief of Detectives was not satisfied. "If this was supposed to be a sting, where's your backup?"

"I sent them home," Norah replied. "We'd been sitting here for four nights and nothing was happening. I figured Leclerc was onto us."

"This 'team' is made up entirely of civilians?"

"They used to be police officers, Chief."

Deland merely grunted. "When you came to me with the idea of pretending that Jim had fallen into another coma and then finally died, in order to draw the perp out into the open, I thought it was worth a try. I didn't expect anybody would be shot, or that Jim would have to answer to IA for the shooting."

"No sir, neither did I," Norah said humbly.

"Nothing at all was said about Jim's participation."

"No sir, I didn't intend he should take an active part."

Felix broke in to rescue her. "For the very good reason that no violence was anticipated. I agreed to lie low and stay out of sight for a couple of days. Sally agreed to handle the media and play the part of the grieving widow—after all, she was an actress. We expected it to be all over fast."

"So what happened? How did you come to be here?" Deland asked.

"When the lieutenant presented her plan to me, I had qualms. I was particularly concerned about the reliability of her backup. Were these men she was working with physically capable of acting as backup? Could they protect her? I wanted to put younger and stronger men on the detail. But she insisted that the more people who knew what we were up to, the more chance there was that word of my being alive would get out. So we made a deal: she would call me every hour. When she didn't, I came over. Just in time, thank God."

Deland frowned. He was a veteran, risen through the ranks and vastly respected by the men and women under him, as by the general public. He was not averse to allowing creative detective work occasionally, but he gave nobody carte blanche. He shifted the unlit cigar from one side of his mouth to the other while he contemplated. "I take it you're prepared to connect all this to the Blue Deaths, Lieutenant?"

"Yes, Chief," Norah replied.

Deland grunted, "And it's a long story, I suppose."

"Yes, sir."

"All right. I'll hear it in the morning—my office, ten o'clock. Jim, I'll give you a lift home." The Chief took one more look at the signs of the violence that had taken place in Norah Mulcahaney's bedroom: the chalk outline of the body, now removed, the large dark areas of white carpet soaked with the perp's blood. Like a bloodhound, the Chief lowered his head and with his large nose sniffed at the scent.

"You can't sleep here, Lieutenant."

"I'll bunk with my son."

"Ah yes . . . Christopher."

"Patrick."

"Of course. He's the cause of all this brouhaha. Unwittingly," he hurried to add.

"No sir, he's not. He has nothing to do with any of it."

"We'll discuss that in the morning."

▼ Police procedure required that every shooting of a civilian by an officer be reviewed by the Internal Affairs Bureau. So Norah was not surprised to find Detective Oscar Farnum already seated in the C of D's office when she arrived. Farnum was in his mid-thirties, wore a conservative business suit and metal-rimmed glasses. He had a narrow, pinched face, and despite the glasses, squinted frequently. He reminded Norah of nearly every IA man she'd ever met.

Luis Deland performed the introductions genially and briskly, but Farnum did not respond in a like manner. His handshake, performed because Deland indicated it was expected, was limp—anything but enthusiastic.

Jim Felix arrived moments later and the perfunctory ceremony was again performed. Felix then kissed Norah on the cheek and took a chair beside her while Detective Farnum sat removed from them on the far side of Deland's desk. The arrangement seemed to please the man from IA. He accepted the offer of coffee, but didn't wait for it to arrive before getting down to business.

He took a file folder from his briefcase. "Give us a brief outline of the case, Lieutenant."

Norah had expected to be called on for this and was prepared.

"I entered the case with the apparent suicide of Sergeant Kevin Douglas," she began. "As we all know, there had been a rash of suicides among police officers and Commissioner Lundy was worried. There appeared to be no motivation for any of them. Particularly it seemed strange that Kevin Douglas, an outstanding officer, decorated and carrying more honors than any officer on the force, should kill himself at the time of his greatest success. Chief Felix suggested I visit Douglas's widow, Ellen Douglas, to offer condolences and get an impression of the situation."

"It was Chief Felix's idea you should do this?" Farnum asked.

"That's right."

"Why don't we wait till Lieutenant Mulcahaney is finished with her report," Deland suggested.

Norah continued. "I discovered that the Douglases were having marital difficulties and that there was a strong possibility that Kevin Douglas was having an affair with the wife of another police officer. It seemed to me there was more motive for murder than suicide. Douglas could have been killed by his lover, her husband, or his own wife, Ellen, had she found out what was going on.

"Later, when we made the connection between the Blue Deaths and Jean-Marie Leclerc, we were able to confirm that Douglas was not one of them."

"A separate investigation into his murder was begun," Deland announced. "We now believe Douglas was killed by the man who was in love with Douglas's wife, Ellen. A man who was a family friend, who rode with him, his partner of four years—Dave Hinkley."

Norah's mouth dropped open. Fortunately, no one noticed. Why hadn't someone told her?

"Hinkley loved Mrs. Douglas and couldn't bear to see her hurt and humiliated by Douglas's actions. And we didn't tell you, Lieutenant, because we didn't want you wasting any more time on it. We considered the case closed and wanted Sergeant William Ciccerone to be the focus of your attention."

"He already was, sir." Norah allowed only the slightest hint of disappointment to show.

"Among Sergeant Ciccerone's effects, we found newspaper accounts of Jean-Marie Leclerc's trials, his ultimate conviction, and his release. That told us what to look for and where to look for it."

"That's for background, Detective Farnum," Deland said. "Details of last night's shooting speak for themselves."

Farnum was not cowed. "It seems strange that none of the victims, including yourself, Chief"—he bowed his head in acknowledgment of Jim Felix's rank—"discerned the connection between Leclerc and the men he killed. Shouldn't at least one of the witnesses at Leclerc's trial have recalled his threats?"

"Do you recall every threat made against you over the years?" Deland asked, still maintaining his mild, almost genial manner. "If cops and lawyers took every threat seriously, they'd lock their doors at night and never come out in the daylight."

"We're not concerned with generalities, Chief Deland." Farnum was persistent. "Whether or not any one of the victims was aware of who was pursuing him, or why, is not at issue—in this inquiry. There is only one question that has to be asked and needs to be answered—by you, Chief Felix."

Jim Felix straightened in his chair and looked directly at his interrogator, his face stoic.

Norah held her breath.

"You said you fired to protect Lieutenant Mulcahaney."

"That's right."

"Why did you fire four times? Surely one shot would have sufficed? According to your own testimony, the first shot hit Leclerc's hand."

"But he didn't drop the gun."

"The second shot hit him in the left shoulder. The third all but destroyed his face. The fourth struck his heart."

Felix gripped the arms of his chair until his knuckles went white. A tremor passed through his body. He had to clear his throat twice. "I admit those shots were not necessary. I lost control. The man who stood before me was covered not only with his blood but with the blood of an untold number of innocent victims. To me, his refusal to drop the gun he held pointed at Lieutenant Mulcahaney indicated both cowardice and arrogance. I lost control." Felix bowed his head.

Norah released her breath.

Chief Deland took the ever present cigar out of his mouth and placed it to one side in an ashtray.

"Personal motivations don't count," he declared. "The crux of what happened is that the perp did not drop his gun when ordered to do so by a police officer. He did not drop it after the first shot, nor the second, nor the third or fourth. He went down with the gun still in his hand."

▼ The media had a field day with it. Reporters staked out both the Felixes' apartment building and Norah's. Television vans and their crews clogged the streets while they waited for anyone with any connection to the case to appear. It got so bad that Sally and Jim Felix flew off to Nassau for a week of R and R.

Bringing Patrick home at last, Norah had to sneak him and Mrs. Gantry in through the back. Meanwhile, Renquist and his buddies worked the talk show circuit to their profit and pleasure. They were having the time of their lives. It wasn't possible to turn on the TV without encountering one of their smiling, eager faces; they basked in the glow of the publicity that others shunned. Rather than waste it—it was beyond price—they decided to go into business for themselves and reap the rewards. They set up their own PI agency. It seemed their "five minutes of fame" would last forever. Suddenly, Norah had time for Patrick. What she needed was to get back to work. But she hadn't solved her domestic problem. She acknowledged she had not been trying recently, and the reason was a nagging doubt she kept pushing to the back of her mind but which refused to stay there.

A call from Manny Jacoby at the Two-Oh, and the return of Jim and Sally Felix from what Jim referred to as a second honeymoon, forced her to take action.

▼ Felix came out of his private office to greet Norah. He looked tanned and fit. He seemed to have gained weight and taken off years.

"I don't want to be disturbed," he told his secretary. "No calls unless the building is on fire."

As Felix held the door and Norah passed by, Paula Lawson cast her a look that was both admiring and envious.

Felix closed the door and indicated a chair.

"I wondered when you'd come," he said.

Norah noted he hadn't said "if." "We need to talk."

"Yes."

Obviously he wasn't going to volunteer anything. He was waiting for her to make the case without his help.

"I've tried very hard, but there are certain things I don't understand," Norah told him. "To start with, you say you don't remember Leclerc, but you were a witness for the prosecution."

"That was eight years ago. Do you remember—"

"Yes, I do. That was the year Joe was killed. I wanted to resign.

You talked me out of it. I went to live in the Amish country, temporarily. I had no idea what was happening here. I didn't care."

"Sorry. I didn't mean to stir up—"

"I also wonder why you weren't called upon to testify in the first two trials. Why did the DA wait till the third time around to call you?"

"You'll have to ask him to explain his strategy."

With each exchange the gulf between them widened. They had never been antagonists before. It distressed Norah, but she persisted. "You were the only additional witness in that third trial. It had to be your evidence that convicted Leclerc. And you don't remember? You have to remember."

"Sorry. I don't."

Norah took a deep breath and plunged. "Leclerc was released seven months ago and since then he's been calling attention to himself by his demands. You must have been aware that he was awarded four hundred thousand dollars in his case against the FBI, and he's also filed against the Department of Correction and the NYPD. That should have reminded you." She modified her tone to match his. "It's not credible that you don't remember, Jim. It just isn't."

"It is to everyone but you," he retorted bitterly. "All right, all right. I knew Leclerc had been released. I expected to be harassed by phone calls, more threats, stalked even, but nothing happened. I figured the money was keeping him happy."

"And you didn't alert the others?"

"There was no reason to. At least, I didn't think so."

"Didn't it worry you when they started dying off, one after the other?"

"Everything pointed to their having committed suicide. It wasn't till you investigated the Douglas death that the possibility of murder came up."

"Is that why you bought the book on voodoo?"

"If I told you it came in the mail, unsolicited . . ."

"Not good enough."

"The same way as the drug-laced aftershave? And your face cream?" Felix reminded her.

Norah considered. "That would mean Leclerc wanted you to know what was in store for you. He wanted you to know you were going to die, but he wanted you to suffer first, wanted to destroy your spirit." She paused. "Why didn't he do the same to the others?"

"It was my direct evidence in the third trial that finally nailed him."

They shared a moment of silence, two old friends who could never be friends again.

"Try to understand the position I was in back then," Felix said. "The district attorney was prosecuting certain black terrorists and they put out a contract on him. Police protection was set up around the clock. I had recently been appointed inspector and was assigned to head up a task force. To start with, it was not my field of expertise. Also, I had been doing supervisory work too long. . . . the job itself would usually have gone to a lower-ranking officer, but there was a diplomatic connection, so I couldn't afford to try and duck it.

"I set it up by the book: two men with the DA at all times. Two on guard at his office, front and rear entrances; two at his home, front and rear; two inside.

"Then when the jury deliberations began, we got word through a snitch that if the verdict was guilty, there would be an attempt on the prosecutor's life. So we beefed up our force and waited. We were all pretty tense and anxious to get it over. You know the feeling."

Only too well, Norah thought.

"The DA's residence was located on the Upper East Side on an elegant, quiet street. You're familiar with the area. You live nearby."

"Yes."

"Well, the verdict came in and it was guilty—as anticipated. We were ready, we thought, but we hadn't expected they would attack with such violence and in numbers and in broad daylight. We had envisioned one or at most two assassins stealthily seeking entrance.

But they came like an assault force at the time we were changing shifts, which was when we were most vulnerable. The arrogance of it!" Felix shook his head.

"I was on the street at the time overseeing deployment of the new men. I noticed the panel van as it turned the corner at what seemed a very slow speed. Before I had time to speculate, it stopped, the back doors opened, and six men jumped out. They were wearing ski masks and carrying semiautomatics. They opened fire as soon as they hit the ground. Following the truck as it cleared the way for them, they strutted down the middle of the street strafing indiscriminately. They worked with disciplined precision. We were completely disorganized. It would have been an episode out of the Keystone Kops if it weren't that four people were killed. We tried to pick them off, but we only had handguns, and civilians kept getting in the way. When at last sirens indicated help was near, they jumped into the waiting van and sped away. All but one."

"Leclerc," Norah said. "He was wounded?"

"In the leg. Nothing."

"Leclerc charges that important evidence was withheld at his various trials, evidence that would have cleared him of the shootings. What evidence?" Norah asked.

"The bullets recovered from the slain officers' bodies. They didn't come from Leclerc's gun."

Norah gasped. She looked at James Felix in disbelief. "The bullets came from *your* gun! You killed those people. You shot them down, not Leclerc."

"They stepped into the line of fire. It was an accident. You've got to believe that."

"That's not what you said at the trial. According to the transcript, you testified that you saw Leclerc raise his gun directly at the two officers, but you weren't quick enough to stop him." Norah paused. "You lied. Why? You could have explained as you did to me. Why didn't you explain?"

"I was ready to tell the truth, but it was my first major assignment, and I blew it. I allowed the terrorists to escape. Four people were dead and all I had to show for it was Leclerc. He wouldn't talk; he wouldn't tell us who he was working for or who set up the operation. He was useless."

Norah wasn't really listening. "You also shot the two civilians, didn't you? Deliberately."

"Why would I do that?"

"Because they could testify that you had shot those two cops." Norah was deeply saddened.

"It was friendly fire. It happens. I regretted it, believe me, but . . . it happens."

"So you just let it go? All these years . . ."

"Don't you get it? Don't you understand? They didn't want me to tell the truth. The State Department and the Haitian government were engaged in some delicate negotiations. State wanted Leclerc to be convicted; they wanted him branded as a terrorist—which he certainly was."

"Who told you that?"

"Nobody told me. It was intimated in a couple of interviews I had with their people." Felix paused to see how Norah was taking all this. "It was strongly suggested that I let matters stand. The longer I agonized over it, the harder it got to make a clean breast of it. Now, it's too late. It would make everybody look bad, and what use would it be?"

"How could you let an innocent man be convicted and go to prison for eight years?"

"He was not an innocent man!" Felix cried out. "He was there. He took part in an armed assault. And Jean-Marie Leclerc was guilty of brutal, sadistic, unspeakable crimes in his homeland before he even came here. Have you any idea what life was like under the Duvaliers in Haiti? Do you know what crimes the *tonton macoutes* committed? What does it matter what he's punished for as long as he is punished?"

Norah shook her head. "The decision wasn't for you to make."

She sighed. "All these years, all your success, your career—all built on a lie."

"It was the one and only time, I swear."

"We admired you, Joe and I. You were our ideal, our role model. We would have done anything for you."

"I never intentionally harmed anyone—not then and not now."

"What about Detective Schiff and Sergeant Ciccerone? And the others before them? Did you at least warn them about what you suspected was happening? No, you left them vulnerable to a madman. You were afraid they might reveal your ugly little secret, so you let him silence them for you. You are as guilty of their deaths as if you'd introduced the drug into their blood and placed the barrel of their own guns into their mouths."

Jim Felix blanched. He had returned from Nassau tanned and healthy-looking, eyes bright. In the past few minutes all that had been swept away.

"I played right into your hands, didn't I." It was a statement rather than a question. "My plan to trap Leclerc was just what you were looking for. It suited you perfectly. It presented you with the opportunity not only to commit murder and get away with it, but to look like a hero for saving my life." Norah slowly shook her head. "You didn't need to shoot four times; Leclerc was already finished. It was overkill, Chief."

Felix sagged visibly. He might have challenged that; instead he asked a favor. "Will you give me a couple of days? I need to tell Sally and to make arrangements."

They looked at each other—old friends who could never again believe in each other. Norah didn't ask what arrangements.

"Two days, no more."

▼ Precisely forty-eight hours later, Police Commissioner Peter Lundy called a news conference for noon, at which time an important announcement would be made. Oddly enough, there were no leaks regarding the subject matter, so as the time approached, curiosity became intense. The event was to be carried on New York 1, the city's cable channel, and Norah decided that rather than try to find a seat in the auditorium, she would watch the press conference from home.

Promptly on the hour the red lights on the cameras lit up, indicating that they were on the air.

Police Commissioner Lundy followed by two chiefs, Deland and Felix, walked out on the stage. He strode to the microphone while they kept slightly back and to one side. The noise and small talk was instantly stilled. Curiosity was about to be satisfied.

Commissioner Lundy cleared his throat.

"Ladies and gentlemen . . ." He waited till there was complete silence. "Thank you. We have just come through a trying, stressful time during which the mettle of this department has been sorely tested. Despite the great strides made recently in cutting down the crime rate to a degree unmatched by any other city or administration, we were faced with a crisis. We experienced a rash of suicides among our people which threatened to dim the success we had achieved.

"Through the work of these two fine men, Chief Deland and Chief Felix, we now know that the suicides were staged."

The reporters stirred; they sensed something really big.

"They were not suicides but murders, cunningly planned and coldly carried out. The victims—Detectives Foxworth and Kramer; Detective Schiff of Internal Affairs; Sergeant Ciccerone, recently retired—were first drugged so that in a semicomatose state each man allowed the barrel of his own service revolver to be placed in his mouth and the trigger to be pulled by his own hand."

A collective sigh passed through the hall. They were shocked, but they wanted more. What a story!

"Chief Felix himself came close to being a victim."

He paused, thus eliciting a generous round of applause.

"I want to commend both these fine men for work well done." Lundy made a half-turn and offered his hand first to Deland and then to Felix. "And to award each one the Combat Cross. Congratulations." With that, he handed Deland and Felix each a small velvet-covered box.

Flashbulbs went off as photographers recorded the simple ceremony, and enthusiastic applause filled the auditorium.

"Now Chief Felix has an announcement to make." The Commissioner made way for Jim Felix to take the microphone.

Norah tensed and leaned forward to her TV set. *Cover-up!* The words shrieked inside her head. Had Deland been in on it? Had he known what had happened and kept silent? How many others were in the conspiracy of silence? Or was the Chief of Detectives allowing Jim Felix to bow out gracefully out of respect for the years of honorable service? But now Felix was at the podium.

"Thank you for your kind words, Commissioner Lundy. I have spent twenty-seven years in the New York Police Department. It has been an honor and a privilege to serve the people of this city, and I had hoped to go on doing so for another twenty-seven years."

A ripple of sympathetic laughter and a smile from Felix himself supported the words. "But for reasons of health, I cannot. Therefore, I now reluctantly tender my resignation."

More flashbulbs.

"My wife, Sally, and I plan to work for the Christian Foundation for Children and the Aging, which has headquarters in Kansas City. We hope, after a period of training, to be sent to one of their missions, perhaps in the Philippines or Africa or Bosnia, wherever the need is greatest."

Norah turned off the set.

Jim Felix had chosen his own penance. Who was she to judge whether it was cheating justice?

▼ Norah knew she could not put off dealing with her household problems much longer. Captain Jacoby was losing patience and she couldn't blame him. She sat at her desk, doodling on the blotter and getting up the nerve to make the call.

Maybe she could arrange to work a regular day shift, eight to four—if Mrs. Gantry would agree to cover those hours on a permanent basis. Norah had never pinned Ida Gantry down to saying why she couldn't work nights or weekends, she'd just been happy to get her when she could. So if Mrs. Gantry was with Patrick days and she was with him the rest of the time, the problem was solved.

She was kidding herself. It wasn't good enough. In hardship cases, a detective might ask for a regular shift and get it, but Norah was head of a division. She had to be available at all times. She never knew when a call might come in the middle of the night and she'd have to dress and go—leaving Patrick alone. A cold chill made her shudder. She hadn't realized until that very moment that she was faced with giving up her job, a job she loved, that she was good at, and that hitherto had filled her life.

She would still have to work, of course. Her retirement benefits wouldn't be enough to cover her and Patrick's needs, particularly looking ahead to college costs. She would have to find another job, a regular job with regular hours.

There were plenty of jobs—no, positions—that she could qualify for, Norah thought as she stared vacantly out the window. There was a big demand for ex–police officers in the security business at all levels: good-paying jobs with regular hours and all kinds of benefits. She had to think of such things now that she was a head of family, and it wasn't fair to keep Manny Jacoby waiting any longer.

She started to dial. A step sounded behind her and she turned to see Ida Gantry at her shoulder. "You startled me."

"I'm sorry. I didn't want to leave before speaking with you. Do you have a few moments? There's something I need to discuss with you."

"Of course, Mrs. Gantry. Please, sit down."

"Thank you, I prefer to stand. This won't take long."

Oh, God! She's going to quit, Norah thought. She's going to say she can't come anymore.

"My niece is going to be married."

"Oh? How nice," Norah murmured automatically, deeply relieved. "Congratulations." She'd be wanting time off, of course. That's what this was all about. If Mrs. Gantry was to be a member of her niece's wedding, that might add up to several days. Well, it couldn't be helped. She'd have to give her the time. She could hardly say no.

"You must be very happy." She'd manage somehow, Norah thought, but it was a reminder of how very fragile the present arrangement was.

Mrs. Gantry had stopped talking and seemed to be waiting for a reply.

"What?" Norah asked. "I'm sorry, I was thinking. What did you say?"

"I said—if you still want me?"

"Want you? What for?"

"To live in. For me to come and live with you and look after Patrick on a permanent basis. Unless you've made other arrangements . . ."

Norah wasn't sure she'd heard right. "Arrangements?"

"For Patrick. It isn't good for the boy to have so many different people around him." She stopped. Planting her feet apart firmly, she began again. "My niece, Alma . . . You remember Alma, my sister Dorothy's child. She inherited the apartment from her mother? I've been sharing it with her."

"Of course, of course."

"Well, Alma is getting married. She and her intended plan to live there. They've invited me to keep my room and live there with them, but I can't do that. If they'd been married a long time, that might be different. But they'll be newlyweds! I can't intrude."

"No, of course not." Norah could see where this was leading and held her breath.

"They're talking about postponing the wedding till I find a place to go."

"No need to look, Mrs. Gantry. You have a place, right here with

Patrick and me. This is great news, Mrs. Gantry. Great news. Patrick will be so happy."

They beamed at each other. Impulsively, Norah got up and went over to embrace the nanny. "What about your night job?"

Despite the heavy white makeup, Ida Gantry flushed. "You knew? How did you find out?"

"I am a detective, Mrs. Gantry. By profession. Actually, you were so obliging in everything else, but so determined on the one point— that you were not available after six P.M.—I had to find out. It required a few questions from your neighbors to confirm my suspicion that you had another job, one you obviously didn't want to give up. What changed your mind?"

"I'm a resident alien. I need to get my green card if I want to go on living and working here. Mercy Hospital hired me and sponsored my application for a green card. I couldn't leave till I got it. With all the recent scandals about celebrities hiring illegal aliens, I was afraid you wouldn't keep me on. I was afraid I might get deported."

"I wish you'd told me. I might have been able to help."

"I didn't want to put any more burden on you. You had so much to worry about."

"I appreciate that, but in the future all problems up front. Okay?"

Mrs. Gantry nodded. "Well, as a matter of fact, there is something." She paused.

"What?" Norah asked.

"I have a cat. Alma's intended is not keen on cats. What shall I do about him?"

Before Norah could answer, Patrick burst into the room.

"His name is Flash because he runs so fast. He's gray all over and he has long white whiskers and yellow eyes and the longest tail you've ever seen. Can Flash come and live with us?"

"Well, I don't know."

Her son stood before Norah and gravely pleaded his cause. "I promise to take care of him. I'll feed him every morning and I'll change his litter. Mrs. Gantry showed me how when I was at her house. I'll brush him and we'll play ball. He swats the ball with his paw. "Oh, Mama, can Flash come and live with us too?

"Please, Mama. Please, please . . ."